BY LARRY MCMURTRY

Literary Life: A Second Memoir
Books: A Memoir
When the Light Goes
Telegraph Days
Oh What a Slaughter
The Colonel and Little Missie
Loop Group
Folly and Glory
By Sorrow's River
The Wandering Hill
Sin Killer
Sacagawea's Nickname: Essays on the American West
Paradise
Boone's Lick
Roads: Driving America's Great Highways
Still Wild: Short Fiction of the American West 1950 to the Present
Walter Benjamin at the Dairy Queen
Duane's Depressed
Crazy Horse
Comanche Moon
Dead Man's Walk
The Late Child
Streets of Laredo
The Evening Star
Buffalo Girls
Some Can Whistle
Anything for Billy
Film Flam: Essays on Hollywood
Texasville
Lonesome Dove
The Desert Rose
Cadillac Jack
Somebody's Darling
Terms of Endearment
All My Friends Are Going to Be Strangers
Moving On
The Last Picture Show
In a Narrow Grave: Essays on Texas
Leaving Cheyenne
Horseman, Pass By

BY LARRY MCMURTRY AND DIANA OSSANA

Pretty Boy Floyd
Zeke and Ned

RHINO RANCH

A NOVEL

LARRY MCMURTRY

SIMON & SCHUSTER PAPERBACKS

New York • London • Toronto • Sydney

SIMON & SCHUSTER PAPERBACKS
A Division of Simon & Schuster, Inc.
1230 Avenue of the Americas
New York, NY 10020

First Simon & Schuster trade paperback edition June 2010

SIMON & SCHUSTER PAPERBACKS and colophon are registered trademarks of
Simon & Schuster, Inc.

For information about special discounts for bulk purchases,
please contact Simon & Schuster Special Sales at
1-800-456-6798 or business@simonandschuster.com

Designed by Dana Sloan

Manufactured in the United States of America

10 9 8 7 6 5 4 3 2 1

The Library of Congress has cataloged the hardcover edition as follows:

McMurtry, Larry
    Rhino ranch : a novel / Larry McMurtry.—1st Simon & Schuster hardcover ed.
        p. cm.
    1. Older men—Fiction. 2. Thalia (Tex. : Imaginary place)—Fiction. 3. City and
town life—Fiction. 4. Regret—Fiction. 5. Texas—Fiction. I. Title.
    PS3563.A319R47 2009
813'.54—dc22   2009019648
ISBN 978-1-4391-5639-1
ISBN 978-1-4391-5640-7 (pbk)

In memory of Luke Smith
and Howard Lyles:
Top Hands

And for James and Curtis,
Top hands in another sphere

PART I

1

BOYD COTTON AND Bobby Lee Baxter—friendly but not yet quite friends—surveyed the faint south plains dawn from their comfortable cots atop Observation Post Number One—in effect the north gate to what, it was hoped, would someday be the world-famous Rhino Ranch.

A species near extinction, the African black rhinoceros, was being transferred in toto to West Texas, where, with luck and skill and lots of money, the species had a chance of being saved.

Boyd Cotton and Bobby Lee Baxter had long known one another well enough to wave, if they happened to meet on the road, but now this noble project—saving the black rhino—had thrown them together professionally. After most of a lifetime as mere nodding acquaintances they were the first two local employees of Rhino Enterprises, and were being paid top hand wages to manage the North Texas end of a very ambitious operation; though, of the two, only Boyd Cotton was a genuine top hand, in cowboying terms. Having spent his life as a much sought-after working cowboy, he had certainly never expected to end up saving rhinos.

But in fact most of the local ranches on which Boyd had often been employed had been chopped up into hunting leases, which meant fewer and fewer jobs for the handful of skilled cowboys that remained. And, though his abilities had not diminished, Boyd was seventy-eight; for him and those few like him, the end of cowboying was not far.

Bobby Lee Baxter—except on divorce papers his last name was seldom used—had scratched out a living in the oil patch, working mostly for his friend Duane Moore, the most prosperous small producer in the area.

The term *top hand,* seldom employed at all, was never employed in the oil patch. Top hands—there had never been many—were always cowboys, on the south plains of Texas.

Despite the hour and the nobility of their great project, Bobby Lee's thoughts drifted off toward what had been a longtime preoccupation: sex.

"Would you believe I've been married twice in the last five years, and that's just in eastern Colorado," he said. "Those are the actions of a dick-driven man. There's days when pussy's pretty much all I can manage to think about. How about you, Boyd?"

"I give more thought to horses—always have," Boyd said. "What I've been applying most of my thought to lately is whether a good well-winded Texas quarter horse could outrun a black rhino, and for how long."

The Rhino Ranch consisted of one hundred and twenty thousand acres of short grass prairie, with a scattering of mesquite thickets and chaparral patches for the rhinos to plod through.

At the moment the only rhino in sight was an old bull named Double Aught, who, as dawn broke, was eating hay out of a hay rack about one hundred yards away. Fourteen more rhinos were off keeping to themselves in various parts of the big pasture. In time, it was hoped, many more would join them.

To the north a soft pink dawn was spreading color along the horizon. The lights of nearby Wichita Falls were just beginning to blink off.

Closer in, not much more than a mile away, Bobby Lee spotted two small fires, deep in the brush land.

"Meth's being cooked," he said, pointing toward the fires.

"That's true, but it ain't being cooked on the Rhino Ranch," Boyd pointed out. "Even a stupid meth head has better sense than to cook their shit where a four-thousand-pound animal could ram a horn as big as a fence post through the cook."

He switched on a cell phone and called the sheriff's office in Thalia, a hamlet four miles away. Soon lights from two police cars were flashing on the road toward the fires.

"I wonder if the meth cookers have figured out that we're the snitches?" Bobby Lee said.

Boyd shrugged. They had both been equipped with powerful rifles, a bullet from which would reduce a meth dealer to a very small smudge.

"You're not much for talking pussy, I guess," Bobby Lee said, as they prepared to climb down from their observation post to go in search of breakfast.

"I like to think I'm still a cowboy," Boyd told him. "Cowboys don't talk about it much. You can't be worrying about your dick if you're working cattle and trying to work them right."

Bobby Lee was undiscouraged.

"I guess you heard I went so far as to have a penile implant," Bobby volunteered. It was a subject he found himself unable to quit talking about, even when his listeners would rather not hear any more about the matter.

Of course Boyd *did* know about Bobby's implant, but he didn't want to enter into conversation about it. He also knew that Bobby had only one testicle, having lost the other to cancer some years ago. He climbed down from the platform and walked over to his pickup, which was not new.

Bobby Lee, however, proved hard to shake.

"People like me—sex addicts I guess you'd say—need support groups," he said. "I doubt I can scrape up much of one in this miserable place, though."

Boyd Cotton's only response was to lean against his pickup and have a smoke.

THE RHINO RANGERS, as Boyd and Bobby were encouraged to call themselves, were not supposed to leave their observation site until the next shift of Rhino Rangers were in place. The next shift, in this case, consisted of the Hartman twins, Bub and Dub, late-nighters who were prone to oversleeping.

Bub and Dub were called the Hartman twins because they had been delivered by their mother and one of her boyfriends during a particularly popular episode of the almost forgotten sitcom *Mary Hartman, Mary Hartman*. Since their unorthodox birth, Bub and Dub had distinguished themselves mainly by growing, tipping the scale at a robust two hundred and sixty pounds apiece.

"Very little of that's brain matter," Bobby Lee had been heard to say, in a caustic tone.

Sure enough when Boyd Cotton called the twins they were sound asleep, but Boyd Cotton's voice had a way of bringing the most comatose sleeper awake—not more than six or seven minutes later the twins came bouncing over the big cattle guard. Their Rhino Ranger T-shirts were not tucked in, but they scurried up the ladder to the observation post with surprising quickness, given their weight.

"I'm told rhinos can move fast too, when they want to," Bobby Lee said. He was tired of trying to make conversation with the mostly unsociable Boyd Cotton, but, unless he wanted to stand around being silent, he had little choice but to try.

"When do you reckon we'll get to meet the boss lady?" he asked, as the two of them got into the heavily reinforced Range Rover they had been assigned and headed north for breakfast, their destination being a nearby crossroads deli run by Mike and Tommy, two hardworking Sri Lankans who had made a go of their unpromising enterprise, the Asia Wonder Deli, where they served tasty fresh spring rolls, crab and barbecued pork to grateful oilfield hands who had previously had to make do with micro-waved burritos.

"Our boss lady's supposed to be a billionairess," Boyd reminded him. "People with that much money are hard to predict. Hell, *I'd* be hard to predict if I had that much money."

"You're hard to predict anyway, Boyd, and your damn pickup's ten years old," Bobby Lee mentioned.

Since their shift was over, Boyd felt no obligation to make conversation with Bobby Lee—especially not before breakfast, which he always looked forward to.

The boss lady Bobby Lee had referred to was a South Texas heiress named K. K. Slater; she was six two, fifty-two years old, preferred to dress as a cowboy and flew her own planes, which included a Cessna and three helicopters. It was said that she brooked no opposition, and suffered fools not at all. She had been brought up in the feudal manner on a very large ranch and was thought to have the habit of command.

So far her only visit to the range she hoped to fill with black rhinos was a quick flyover in her Cessna, on which occasion she came solo.

As they approached the Asia Wonder Deli, Boyd Cotton's mood improved. Bobby Lee often exasperated him, but then most people exasperated him—the likely effect of too many years batching, he supposed.

As usual the Asia Wonder Deli was practically surrounded by muddy pickups, most of them the property of the Moore Drilling Company. The pickups were parked willy-nilly, wherever their drivers could find a spot. Bobby Lee, master of a splendid Range Rover, built to withstand rhino attacks, drove across a small creek and parked on its bank.

"It's about this time of day that I miss old Duane," Bobby Lee said, as the sun rose over the mesquite. "Me and him have probably seen as many sunrises together as any people on the planet."

Boyd didn't really know Duane Moore, though of course, through the years, he had often seen him around. He let Bobby Lee's comment drift away.

"His boy, Dickie, mostly runs the company now," Bobby Lee went on.

"From what I can see here they've got no shortage of pickups," Boyd said.

"Duane's a kind of top hand, like you—only in the oil business," Bobby went on. "You know, the go-to guy."

"Being the go-to guy can get irksome," Boyd said. "You might not always be in the mood to be gone to. Probably why Duane left town."

"Oh no," Bobby Lee said. "He left because that long-legged wife of his didn't want to live here—which is reasonable enough, once you think about it."

Soon they were enjoying an excellent Asian breakfast, after which Bobby Lee dropped Boyd off at his pickup, back at the North Gate. Since the Range Rover was supposed to be for company business only, Boyd gave Bobby Lee a lift into Thalia, where the one stoplight continued to blink and blink.

"If you attempt to force me to eat egg whites I may jump up and rebel," Duane said, good-naturedly. In fact he hated egg whites—in his youth there had even been the belief that the two things that caused blindness were egg whites and masturbation.

Annie, his wife of almost five years, came to the table in a caftan that covered her completely, from neck to ankles. She gave no response to his joking complaint.

They were breakfasting on the deck of their adobe home near Patagonia, Arizona. Doves were cooing, the sunlight was strong and a small covey of Gambel's quail skittered across the deck. Two young coyotes loped along a gulch below the house.

"You won't rebel," Annie said firmly, putting a rosy Texas grapefruit before him. Though nearing thirty, Annie looked about sixteen. Duane was charmed by her, as he had been more or less since the moment they met.

"You can always have all the fruit you want," she reminded him. "Your problems lie in the nonfruit areas."

In their years together Annie and Duane had developed a few codes, which, if followed, kept their marriage fairly harmonious. The all-enveloping caftan indicated that Annie had a lover, which meant a period of chastity for Duane. The fact that they had separate bedrooms made this chaste state easier to tolerate. Duane didn't challenge the arrangement, in part because he knew that Annie was inconsistent and would show up in his bed every few nights anyway, out of a need to be held.

Just before his heart surgery. Duane had nearly died while making love to Annie, an experience that left its mark on both of them. A few years after the operation his potency had returned almost to normal, but the death-fuck, as Annie still referred to it, caused both of them to wonder if he would survive all-out lovemaking. As a result they settled for a kind of stutter-step sex, their fears causing them to miss pleasures they might well have enjoyed.

Annie's present lover, Duane suspected, was a young carpenter they hired to do some repairs around the house. Like most local carpenters he worked shirtless and was nicely bronzed by the Arizona sun. Duane had to reconcile himself to the fact that he himself was only going to get older and less vigorous, whereas golden young carpenters would never be in short supply.

Annie was a topflight geological analyst, who worked, technically, for Duane's son, Dickie. As part of her duties, she went to high-level petroleum conferences all over the world; the conferences provided the opportunity for many brief romances, though Duane didn't think Annie had many brief romances—mainly, he thought, she did her work and came home.

While he was eating his grapefruit one of the Gambel's quail jumped up on the table and made off with a blueberry. Duane liked birds and usually had half a dozen or so milling around his feet when he breakfasted outside. Indeed, the little birds provided a bit of company when Annie was gone. There were times, as he aged, when he felt marginal—the presence of the quail and dove seemed to help a little.

ONE DAY, WITH Annie in Vancouver, Duane had a deeper than usual depression—deep enough that he broke his own rules and called Honor Carmichael, his first psychiatrist, who was retired and was living on Long Island with her slightly crippled girlfriend, a famous American painter.

"That's not a happy voice," Honor said, the moment Duane said her name.

"Are you busy?" he asked, nervously.

Honor laughed. "I'm a kept woman, Duane—and handsomely kept, at that. I'm never again likely to be 'busy,' not in the real sense anyway.

"So why'd you call?" she asked.

"I'm more depressed than I have any reason to be," he admitted.

"And Annie's where?"

"Vancouver."

"Lover?"

"I think she might have something going with a carpenter we hired," he said.

"A common choice," Honor said. "Carpenters are usually good with their hands."

"I don't know whether I should bring it up with her or not," he added.

"Don't you utter a word," Honor said. "She didn't marry you for your tolerance."

"I don't feel that tolerant," he said.

"No, but your love is her safety," Honor said. "It may not always be comfortable for you, but it's important."

"I don't make a good retiree," he said. "I'm not used to sitting on the deck with absolutely nothing to do."

"Then go home for a while," she suggested. "Go back to Thalia and see how you feel."

"What?" Duane said, wondering if he had misheard. Honor had been to Thalia. She knew what was there, and, even more importantly, she knew what *wasn't* there.

"Last time I left home I had the feeling I was leaving for good," he said. "I've had to go back a couple of times because of the oil business and I feel about as marginal there as I feel here. Except for one thing."

"Willy?" Honor guessed.

"That's right, Willy, my favorite grandson."

There was a silence.

"Helping Willy's a good enough reason to go home," Honor said. "Didn't you buy your big house back?"

"I did, it was Dickie's idea," Duane said. "We did it mainly to protect the property from a drug dealer that wanted to use it as his warehouse."

"I only met Willy once, but he seemed like a great kid," Honor said. "Go home and be there in case he needs you."

Duane thought for a minute—the conversation had taken a surprising tack. Willy was growing up fast, and it would be fun to spend more time with him.

"You're never really through with your home, Duane," Honor said. "You sort of can't be."

"I wonder if Annie knows that," he said.

"I don't know anything about her upbringing but the tendency of the rich is to keep on the move. It unsettles their kids, who often grow up feeling they had no real home.

"If I were still a shrink I'd advise that you and I have a few sessions together. I want to hear more about why you feel marginal," Honor said.

"It's the best word I can think of."

"Here's another word you might consider: old," she said. "Many aging people feel marginal, to some degree. For decades they're at the center of things, and then one day they're not. They slip over to the sidelines. They become marginal, and next thing you know they're old."

They didn't talk much longer. As usual, though, Honor Carmichael had told him something that felt true.

5

BOYD COTTON WAS generally held to be the best all-round cowboy in the Thalia region, a distinction he had held for almost sixty years. He had one or two peers among local cowboys, but no superiors.

In any local roundup, if he was available, he did the roping—the premier job. He had always been willing to head into the thorniest thicket, to bring out the wildest and wooliest cattle.

Boyd lived alone in a small, seldom painted frame house that stood on what had been his grandparents' homestead. A time or two he had attempted to lease a hundred acres or so and run a few steers of his own, but mainly, all his life, he had lived on freelance cowboying, a day here, two days there.

But, as ranching slowly died, Boyd found it harder and harder to get work. Often he hauled his quarter horse a hundred miles each way, in order to get a day's cowboying.

Much as he loved cowboying, Boyd Cotton did not delude himself about its future—or lack of it. When Rhino Enterprises showed up and offered him a job, he took it at once, and became, for the first time in his life, a salaried man.

Bobby Lee Baxter, who had always been a salaried man—mostly for Moore Drilling—signed up with Rhino Enterprises the same day as Boyd.

In that part of Texas cowboys and oil people had never mixed particularly well. The cowboys were mounted men when possible, and considered themselves lords of the earth, whereas working on a drilling platform soon drove any innate haughtiness out of a man. Oil workers ended their days covered in oil and mud; many of them were never entirely clean.

Still, since they were—before the twins arrived—the only local employees of Rhino Enterprises, Bobby Lee and Boyd edged into friendship. One day they were high on their platform, contemplating lunch, when a line of trucks loaded with white pipe began to bump through the cattle

13

guard. The truck drivers waved at Boyd and Bobby, and continued on west with their loads.

"Thirty-eight miles of rhino-proof fence she's planning to build," Bobby Lee said. "How many of them big mean rhinos will fit inside thirty-eight miles of fence?"

"When the XIT Ranch existed it had six thousand miles of fence," Boyd reminded him. He enjoyed surprising Bobby Lee with a statistic now and then.

"Yeah, but that was just little scratchy barbed wire," Bobby Lee countered. "It would barely keep in yearlings. This fence they're about to build is supposed to withstand the charge of a bull elephant."

"The day there's a charging bull elephant anywhere in these parts is the day I immigrate to Montana," Boyd said. "I once saw a Hereford bull knock over a cattle truck, since which I've done my best to avoid any of the larger species when they're angry.

"Ever slept with a millionairess?" he asked—it was an abrupt change of subject.

"Not only have I never slept with a millionairess," Bobby Lee said, "I've never slept with a woman who wasn't several hundred dollars in debt, which of course she expected me to take care of for her."

Boyd didn't respond.

"And being the generous soul women seem to know me to be, I always do take care of it, ever damn time."

Boyd Cotton continued to hold his peace.

"And then what happened?" Bobby Lee continued before answering his own question. "Two of the women ran off with hardened criminals, and the third had the bad manners to shoot me in the stomach, which brought me to the very brink of death."

"I may have been wise to mainly stick to horses," Boyd observed.

NOT LONG BEFORE Rhino Ranch began to take shape, Duane, on his son, Dickie's, advice, bought a section of land on a low bluff near the Little Wichita River. Though too small an acreage to run cattle on, it did have a hay shed and a small set of pens. Boyd Cotton kept his two quarter horses on the property. Boyd was still much in demand as an arena director at many local rodeos. If any of the bucking stock got fractious, Boyd could be depended on to move them smoothly out of the arena.

The property was adjacent to another section across the small river. Duane's little frame cabin stood atop a low hill. A decade ago Duane had launched his one-man clean-up crusade against mess and litter along the dirt roads around Thalia from his cabin. Ever since, he had occasionally used the cabin as a refuge in times of inner struggle. For a while he horrified his family and everyone else in the town by parking his pickup and walking everywhere. Then he horrified his kin even more by going into therapy with Honor Carmichael, who made him read Proust and indicated that a bicycle was a handy way to get around.

Buying back his big house to protect it from drug dealers seemed only half right to Duane, though he knew that the local constabulary was hard put even to protect themselves from the same danger. But buying the land below the little bluff seemed entirely fitting. If worst came to worst he could live in his old cabin, or build another on the bluff across the creek.

At times, Duane liked to fish, though at other times fishing bored him. His usual fishing buddy, Bobby Lee, mainly went fishing in order to escape the scorn of whatever mean woman he was hooked up with at the time.

At home in Patagonia, Annie was packing to take her longest trip yet, to Tajikistan, where, soon, the distant country would open the longest pipeline in the world, the event Annie was going to help celebrate. She had halfheartedly asked him to go with her on this trip and when he declined she got angry.

"I don't go to places whose name I can't spell," he said lightly.

"Bullshit," Annie said. "You went to Egypt because fucking Honor Carmichael told you to!"

"But I *can* spell Egypt," he said. It didn't help—despite the fact that he was often jealous himself, he had a tendency to forget about jealousy.

Annie stomped off and no more was said about him visiting Tajikistan. But the night before she left they made love successfully.

"It was because you let me have those two lamb chops for dinner," he said, but Annie had faded into postcoital sleep and didn't answer.

The next morning Duane dropped Annie at the Tucson airport and, a day later, caught his own plane to Dallas/Fort Worth. While he was waiting for his luggage he called Bobby Lee.

"Think the Rhino Ranch could spare you for a night or two of bass fishing?" he asked.

"Why, sure," Bobby said. "We're only riding herd—at least Boyd is—on fifteen rhinos so far. A lot of pipe arrived the other day, which might be a good sign."

On his way home Duane detoured through North Fort Worth and ate a hefty platter of good North Fort Worth barbecue; it made up for a lot of egg whites.

7

WHEN DUANE PULLED up to his big house in Thalia, two men in expensive-looking three-piece suits were waiting for him. A black SUV with "Rhino Enterprises" painted on the side was parked by the garage.

"Well, if you're Duane Moore, then I guess we didn't miss you, after all," the taller man said.

"You came close, though," Duane said. "If I had stopped in Jacksboro for a milk shake, like I usually do, I wouldn't be here yet. As it is I'm here but I don't know why you need to see me."

The tall man handed him a nicely designed Rhino Enterprises business card.

"There's a long version, sir, but the short version is that Rhino Enterprises wants to buy your house," the stockier of the two men said.

"I've no interest in selling you my house—or anybody my house," Duane said. He knew the two were land men—he had dealt with hundreds like them while he was running his oil company. Land men were by nature aggressive. He didn't hold it against them but he didn't intend to let it delay him, either.

"Besides that, I've traveled a long way and am in a hurry to get off on a fishing trip," he said. "Meeting's over."

"We work for K.K. Slater," the tall man said. "K.K.'s philosophy is that everything's for sale. It's kind of a working principle for her."

"I guess I'm the exception that proves the rule, because my house isn't for sale," Duane said. "I'm afraid your boss will just have to live with that."

"We're also interested in that section of land you bought on the Little Wichita River," the stubby fellow said.

"That's also not for sale and now I'm going to pick up a few lures and go fishing," Duane said.

He unlocked his house and went in, leaving the two land men standing on his patio. By the time he washed his face and began to collect his tackle the land men in the black SUV were gone.

Though he had vanquished the land men easily enough this time, Duane knew that the rodeo wasn't over. A new force had come into the county, a force so rich that its representatives assumed they could just keep raising the financial ante until they got what they wanted.

A call to his son, Dickie, did nothing to dilute that impession.

"Sure, they came here first," Dickie told him. "Burton and Norm—the tall one's Burton but the shrewd one is Norm. They'd be happy to have your house but what they really want is that section by the river—tourists could sit on that little bluff and watch the rhinos at play just across the road."

"Yeah, but there's one hundred and twenty thousand acres across the road," Duane pointed out. "What if the rhinos don't want to stand around and be gawked at?"

"I expect they're counting on Boyd Cotton or somebody to sort of ease a few rhinos over by the paying guests," Dickie said.

"Well, Boyd could probably manage that," Duane admitted.

"That's not what Norm actually said, it's just my deduction," Dickie said. "They're going to build a world-class veterinarian facility somewhere on the property—a place you could take a sick hippo, if you had one."

"A sick hippo—this is making me dizzy," Duane said.

Dickie chuckled. "It's making the whole county dizzy," he said. "There used to just be millionaires to contend with, but now there's *billionaires*, Daddy—nearly a thousand of them in America and probably more than that in Russia."

Duane let that soak in.

"Have you met K.K. Slater yet?" he asked.

"I sure have," Dickie said. "And I do think she's serious about wanting to save the black rhino.

"Other than that, I don't know what to think," Dickie admitted. "Good luck with the fishing."

WHILE BOBBY LEE was gathering up his fishing gear, a task that took longer than it should have because Bobby couldn't immediately find his lure box or the one dozer cap that he thought brought him good luck, Duane considered calling Tajikistan, where Annie was, but he wasn't sure he had the time difference right and the last thing he wanted to do was wake up his very likely jet-lagged wife.

So he compromised, as he had so often lately: he called Honor Carmichael.

"We're not having phone sex, not now and not ever," Honor said, with a chuckle.

"I wouldn't even know how to start phone sex," Duane said. In fact the idea shocked him.

"You barely know how to do real sex, either," Honor said, lightly.

"Do you know K.K. Slater?" he asked—Honor was the only person he knew, other than his wife, who might move in billionairess circles of the sort K.K. Slater probably moved in.

"I saw her at a polo match once, but that was at least twenty years ago," Honor said. "Of course I read about that Save-the-Rhino project she's doing somewhere in your part of the country. Is it really happening?"

"Seems to be," Duane said. "Bobby Lee works for her and so does a cowboy I know."

"You're using me like the Social Register," she added.

"That's because you're the only person I know who's *in* a Social Register," he said.

"Not so. Both your daughters are in the Dallas Social Register—I keep a copy handy because my gifted girlfriend sells a painting in Dallas, now and then.

"Being in the Social Register is not exactly a crime," Honor said.

"I don't really understand why there needs to be a Social Register, much less why my daughters are in one," he admitted.

"Have you met K.K. yet?" Honor asked.

"No, but she tried to buy my house, and also a little piece of land I own out by the Rhino Ranch," he told her.

"I see," Honor said.

"See what?"

"She wants something you own, and you won't sell," Honor said.

"Correct."

"Well, this might be interesting," Honor said.

10

DUANE AND BOBBY LEE, having been fishing buddies for more than thirty years, were well used to one another's behavior in a boat. In the main their ways were quiet ways. Conversation would be minimal for long stretches, and sometimes it didn't occur at all. When Bobby Lee was in a rowdy mood he went to honky-tonks, not lakes. In honky-tonks there were like to be women who might appreciate his wit, when he could summon any.

Duane considered that he lacked even a smudge of rowdiness—at least various women had mentioned this lack to him.

Neither man applied himself very seriously at first to the serious sport of bass fishing. Thus it came as a huge shock to both of them when Bobby Lee hooked a large bass and brought it into the boat.

Bobby Lee was so stunned by his achievement that he was, for a time, speechless. The fish tipped the scale at sixteen pounds.

"This has got to be the luckiest day of my life, unless you count the day that mean Odessa woman shot me," he said finally.

"What's so lucky about being shot by a mean Odessa woman?" Duane asked.

"She didn't hit no vital organs, that's what," Bobby Lee reminded him.

The rest of the day was spent exhibiting Bobby Lee's great catch to the little community of Possum Kingdom, where the lake was, and the larger community of Graham, a town nearby. Newspapers from as far away as Olney sent photographers, and television crews from two local stations soon showed up.

The reaction of the press left little doubt that big bass were newsworthy in the Possum Kingdom area.

To all these celebrants Bobby Lee was courtesy itself, while remaining modest to a fault. Duane put up with this hubbub mainly because, for once, he got to see his lifelong friend take on a kind of shine. It was the shine of the successful man, and Duane was really happy to see it because for much of his life Bobby Lee had exhibited the resignation of the defeated man. Or, when he didn't actually look defeated, he wore the grim look of a man who was barely holding his own.

At one point Duane left Bobby Lee to his happy audience and rowed across the lake, where he caught two three-pounders and a gar. Hooking a gar was always a nuisance, but Duane had hooked many in his time and knew how to get rid of it.

The record sixteen-pounder got taken to a taxidermist, and, later, Duane and Bobby Lee made a meal off the two three-pounders Duane had caught.

"I guess this means you're going to be the envy of the bass fishing world," Duane said. "Next thing you know they'll be inviting you to Caracas and other places where they have these fancy fishing competitions."

"Well, that wouldn't ncessarily be bad," Bobby said. "Maybe I'll find me a fiery little Latina."

"They say Latinas have a lot of spice," he added. "There's none too much spice to be found around Thalia, these days."

"I don't know if you've noticed but there are Latinas closer than Caracas," Duane reminded him.

"The whole Midwest is filling up with Latinas," Duane said.

"Right, and the Southwest was already full to the brim," Bobby Lee said. "It's a wonder I ain't already married a Latina, if you stop and think about it."

They sat in silence for a while. They had cooked the bass over a little campfire at the edge of the lake. While they watched, a heron landed, and the frogs began to croak.

"Some women have gentler qualities," Duane mentioned—he didn't know why.

Bobby Lee didn't answer, but he continued to shine. After all, he had caught his record bass.

11

A FEW DAYS BEFORE Duane was due to fly back to Arizona to meet Annie on her return, he decided to address himself to a problem that had long vexed him. It involved two corner post holes on the set of pens he owned north of Thalia. The corner posts had initially been set by Dickie, when he was a recovering drug addict, and neither was correctly set. They looked like two small Leaning Towers of Pisa, a reproach to Moore discipline, at least as Duane practiced it. The time had come to reset those posts.

He was at the site of the transgressions at dawn, equipped with two fine bois d'arc posts that, if firmly and accurately set, would last forever, if not longer. It took Duane only a short while to winch the old posts out of the ground. For small jobs such as this one he preferred to work alone, to avoid the chatter that most fencing operations produced. He took his time, enjoying his own ability and cheered by the lack of interference. Only three pickups full of roustabouts had come by, and one lone cowboy, Boyd Cotton, who was on horseback and clearly looking for something.

"I hope there's not a rhino on the loose," Duane said. "I'm busy and would prefer not to be attacked."

"Oh no, all our rhinos are accounted for," Boyd said. "But we're missing our nilgais—eight in number. I hope some damn trigger-happy roughneck didn't amuse himself by shooting a harmless antelope."

"I've never sampled nilgai," Duane said. "I hear they're pretty tasty."

"They have a calming effect on the rhinos," Boyd told him. "That's why we have 'em, and nobody better not shoot one. You going to the speech?"

"What speech?"

"The boss lady's," Boyd said. "She's gonna explain why we need to save the rhino. I *was* going, but then the nilgai turned up missing."

"I've never quite understood ecology," Duane said. "A speech by K.K. Slater might soar right over my head."

"Mine too," Boyd said. He rode off and was back in fifteen minutes, driving the eight missing antelope.

"Some meth dealer cut our fence," he said—"probably one from out of state. The locals know enough to do their cooking on the side of the road where the rhinos ain't."

He left to drive the nilgai home, and Duane went on with his work. In an hour or a little more the corner posts were set the way they should have been set to begin with. He wondered if his old friend Jenny Marlow was attending the rich lady's speech. Jenny was mildly virtuous when it came to the environment. She took her recycling all the way to Wichita Falls—no facilities for recycling were yet available in Thalia.

For much of his life Thalia had mostly depressed Duane, but lately he had developed a kind of tolerance for it. Maybe it was just that as the funeral bell came closer to tolling for him he felt a tendency to linger in what had been, or maybe still was, home.

MOST OF THE antelope of various kinds that Boyd Cotton found himself responsible for had never set foot in Africa, or Asia, or anywhere else other than Texas. They had been purchased at the numerous exotic game auctions that were held frequently in the Hill Country west of Austin. Dik-diks, sable antelope, nilgai and kudus were purchased and brought to the Rhino Ranch to help convince the rhinos that they were still, in a sense, at home.

The liaison man between K.K. Slater's ranching empire to the south, and Boyd and Bobby Lee in Thalia, was a genial Australian named Myles Vane. Myles operated out of Kingsville, Texas, and usually showed up in Thalia whenever K.K. did, and in fact just had.

Boyd Cotton drove the nilgai in the direction that would take them to their normal pasturage; then he rode back to the compound beside the North Gate, meaning to unsaddle his horse. As he dismounted he noticed a tall woman dressed in khaki, wearing a small Stetson that showed a certain amount of grime. He realized then that he was looking at his boss.

And, as it happened, his boss was also looking at him.

"That cowboy can sit a horse," K.K. observed, as Boyd trotted over their way.

"That's Boyd Cotton," Myles said. "He was the top hand in these parts, in his day."

K.K. Slater gave her foreman a caustic look which took him pretty much off guard, though he had long since recognized that it was best to stay on guard when around K.K. Slater.

"From what I can see it's still his day," she said, before walking over to shake hands with Boyd.

"Howdy," Boyd said. If he was surprised it didn't show.

"If you've got the time I'd like you to show me my property," K.K. said.

"Happy to," Boyd said.

A young Latino groom walked over leading a sorrel thoroughbred named Haley, whether after the comet or the historian Boyd didn't know. This time it was Boyd who offered the caustic look.

"Something wrong, cowboy?" K.K. asked.

"Thoroughbred horses make me edgy," Boyd admitted. "You won't find one in fifty you can trust—they're bred too high."

K.K. gave a hearty laugh. "You're not only a top hand, you're a horse philosopher. And you're right—they're bred too high, and they're scary. That's why rich people ride them, if you follow me."

She mounted easily and they set off.

"For rich people there's no kick if it's too safe, and that applies to marriages and oil deals and big game hunting and horses."

They let that subject rest and picked up the pace a little.

"I'm mostly interested in seeing the water holes," she said. "I suspect we'll have to add a few, or else get some windmills."

As they were trotting along near the fence Boyd saw Duane go by in his little white pickup—he was headed in the direction of Thalia.

K.K., who had never met Duane, didn't notice, and immediately asked Boyd if he knew Duane Moore.

"That was him in the white pickup that just went by," Boyd said. "I know him just to wave to, mostly—we're in different lines of work."

"He won't sell me his house and he didn't come to my speech," she said; she sounded not so much angry as curious.

"He was putting in two corner post holes this morning," Boyd said. "Duane's the sort that, if he plans something, he likes to carry it through."

"I have the same inclination," K.K. said. "If you had to describe Mr. Moore in one word what would it be?"

"Competent," Boyd said. When he looked across at K.K. their eyes were on the same level—unusual in his case. K.K.'s eyes, inscrutable behind her sunglasses, were on a level with his. It didn't necessarily mean anything but it was a surprise.

13

THE DOOR TO Jenny Marlow's house had never been locked, or even latched—not in Duane's experience, and he had been visiting the Marlows with some regularity for more than fifty years. Jenny's one and only husband, and Duane's banker and friend, Lester Marlow, had dropped dead at a flea market in Canton, Texas, about two years earlier.

Lester Marlow was more or less crazy, and long had been, but he and Jenny had been part of Duane's life for a long time—long enough that it seemed odd to arrive at the Marlow house and not see Lester wandering around the yard in his bathrobe, shooting at lined-up dominoes with his BB gun. Rarely did he manage to hit the lead domino, which would have caused the whole thing to topple, but he kept trying. In the last years of his life Lester was seldom without his BB gun, and, if he was without it, it was because he was about to head off to a swap meet like the one he died at.

At least Lester kept trying, and so did his long-suffering wife, Jenny, too. Not only did she keep trying with Lester, but she tried with Bobby Lee too. When Bobby Lee's mean Odessa wife shot him in the stomach it was Jenny Marlow who raced over and kept Bobby Lee alive until the none too snappy Thalia ambulance arrived.

Why a woman as competent and appealing as Jenny Marlow put up with someone as incompetent as Lester was just one of the mysteries of life.

When Duane knocked, Jenny came to the door wearing shorts, sandals and a faded T-shirt with "Party Till You Puke" stenciled on it.

The T-shirt gave Duane a real shock, because it had once belonged to his wife, Karla, who had been killed in a head-on collision with a milk truck more than a decade ago.

Jenny let him in and gave him a big hug. She noticed Duane's reaction to the T-shirt, and grinned, showing impressive Duchess of Windsor molars.

27

"Honey, how the hell did you get Karla's T-shirt?" he asked—he wasn't angry, just startled.

"At that big garage sale your daughters held when you sold your house," Jenny told him.

"I wanted to have something to remember Karla by, and what better than a T-shirt with her motto on it?"

Duane thought Jenny looked a little wan.

"Are you okay?" he asked.

"Not entirely," Jenny admitted. "I somehow managed to pick up the Big C. I think I'm gonna beat it, but with the Big C you never know."

"The Big C where?"

"Ovaries," Jenny said. "But enough about me. What brings you here? You've started coming home more often than you used to."

"Well, my wife's in Russia, or what used to be Russia, and I guess I'm just at loose ends," he admitted.

There was a silence, as the old friends contemplated one another. Then Jenny took Duane into the kitchen and poured him some iced tea.

"That little bride of yours travels a lot," Jenny observed. "But it's good to have you, even if it's aberrational behavior on your part. I guess by now you've heard about the Rhino Ranch."

"The rhinos are welcome, as far as I'm concerned," he said. "Maybe a few big scary critters is just what this place needs."

"I meant to go to K.K. Slater's speech but I had chemo yesterday and that'll keep you from doing your civic duty," Jenny said.

Duane didn't answer. He knew ovarian cancer was a serious matter and he thought how desolate Thalia would be without Jenny's fighting spirit.

"I'm real glad you took Bobby Lee fishing," Jenny said. "Catching that prize bass was the high point of his life.

"I suppose that's a sad comment, but it was a fine fish," Jenny said.

"A fine fish for sure," Duane echoed.

DUANE STEPPED INTO the Dairy Queen to get a cheeseburger and immediately spotted his two daughters, Julie and Nellie—they were having salads, though both of them knew perfectly well what grim materials went into salads in Thalia.

Duane had not been surprised to see the girls, since Nellie's Lexus was parked outside. Both daughters jumped up and hugged him. Nellie, as usual, sported a lot of eye makeup, while Julie contented herself with several jangly bracelets.

"What brings you girls to this sunny abode?" he asked. Both at the time were living the life of rich divorcees in North Dallas.

"We came to support K.K. Slater, of course," Julie said. "We're both on the board of Rhino Enterprises, you know—I'm sure K.K. would just be thrilled if you'd come on too. She said herself there's no one she'd rather have."

"Me?" he said. "I can't quite see myself as a boardroom type."

He liked seeing his daughters and didn't want to pick a fight with them. Both seemed a little overdressed, but that had been the case for a long time. Neither of them looked very happy, board or no board.

"It's just that people around here respect you so, Daddy," Julie said. "You're probably the most respected man in this whole part of the country."

"Besides that, you know how people are, around here," Nellie added. "They're just real biased against outsiders. Unless you were born and raised here, they just don't trust you. K.K.'s from somewhere else—they may think they like the notion of the Rhino Ranch but the minute you get down to brass tacks there'll be a lot of opposition."

Duane couldn't argue with that assessment. People from Thalia were severely biased against people not from Thalia. People setting up a business who weren't really *from* the town were at a fatal disadvantage. Bobby

Lee himself, if he needed a new wrench, would cheerfully drive the twenty miles to Wichita Falls and buy one from Target rather than patronize the new but perfectly adequate hardware store in Thalia. Of course in Wichita Falls he dealt with perfect strangers but at least they weren't trying to invade his hometown proper.

Duane himself hated the boring drive to Wichita Falls, a city that now nurtured no fewer than three Wal-Mart Supercenters; he bought as much locally as he could.

"You're right, honey," he said to Nellie. "People here are just real biased against newcomers. But K.K. Slater is not just someone who wants to open a convenience store. She's a billionairess, something the town has never had to deal with before—neither have I, for that matter."

"Please be on her board," Julie asked. "If your name's attached most people will be a little more cooperative."

"Maybe—I can't recall being *that* popular," he said. "Besides, I live in Arizona, which is a fair toot away. I do like the notion of saving the black rhinos, though."

"You always have to argue," Julie said, in a tone that reminded him of her mother, Karla.

"It's just that I'm older," Duane said gently. "I'm cautious about allowing people to expect too much of me. Besides, I don't get home that often."

"No, but you're home now and Willy is coming to see you," Julie said. "He misses his grandpa."

"I'd love to see Willy, when's he coming?" he asked. "Did he come with you girls?"

There was a silence.

"Actually, Willy prefers to hitchhike," Nellie told him.

Julie, whose son Willy was, seemed so embarrassed by this information that she couldn't bring herself to provide it.

"Willy's hitchhiking from North Dallas?" Duane said, astonished.

"He's grown up now, what can I do?" Julie said. "Hitchhiking happens to be his preferred mode of transportation now."

"He'll be welcome if he gets here," Duane said, just as he spotted Boyd

Cotton's old pickup pull in and park. Boyd got out, and so did a woman Duane knew must be K.K. Slater. What brought her to his attention was that she was as tall as Boyd, and Boyd wasn't short.

"Hey, it's K.K.—Daddy will get to meet her at least," Nellie said.

"Is that old Boyd Cotton she's with? I thought he died," Julie said.

"No, don't you remember—he works for Rhino Enterprises," Nellie said. "Please be nice when you meet her, Daddy," Julie pleaded.

Duane wished he had chosen another place to eat, but, except for two convenience stores, there was no other place. And the offers at the two convenience stores were very limited.

"Don't you worry, honey," he said. "I'll be as nice as pie."

15

DUANE STOOD UP to shake hands with K.K. Slater, a courtesy that pleased his daughters no end. Not every diner at the Dairy Queen bothered to stand up when a lady approached.

Boyd Cotton, just as polite, took off his hat and helped K.K. into her seat.

"Hello, girls," K.K. said to Julie and Nellie. "And hello to you, Mr. Moore. I was afraid for a minute that you'd be set on eluding me."

"No, but I'm sorry I missed your speech," he said.

K.K. still wore her glasses.

"Didn't you marry into the Camerons?" she asked.

"Yep," Duane said.

"I've heard your wife is really good at what she does."

"She gets a healthy paycheck, which is about all I know about it," Duane said.

K.K. took off her sunglasses in order to study the menu, a task that didn't take her long.

"They might be out of caviar," Boyd Cotton mentioned, straight-faced.

"Personally I never flinch from a good chicken-fried steak," K.K. said. "It's the staple cuisine of my people—or was until recently. I do insist that it be drenched in cream gravy."

"'Spect they can manage the gravy," Boyd added.

"Don't you think Boyd and I make a nice couple?" she asked, to the surprise of everyone. "We're exactly the same height and both of us devote much of our time to horses. People will be thinking we're an item, if we're not careful."

Boyd Cotton took that in stride. He seemed perfectly at ease with K.K. Slater, a well-educated, sophisticated woman, though he himself had quit school in the fifth grade.

"We've been pestering Daddy with all our might to come be on your board," Julie said, in a tentative tone.

"I'm afraid I'm not much of a hand for boardrooms," Duane said.

"Oh, I wouldn't want you in one of *my* boardrooms," K.K. said, shocking Julie and Nellie. "Your extensive knowledge of Proust—somebody told me you are a devotee—wouldn't help us there. All I want from you is a little help with the locals, if they should get rowdy."

"I'll try, but the fact is the locals pay very little attention to me," Duane said. "I live in Arizona now, which makes me nearly as much an outlander as you are yourself, where the locals are concerned."

"I know—deserters and exiles are rarely welcomed back," K.K. said.

Just then a tall youth, with long but well-combed black hair, wearing a Pearl Jam jacket, walked in—it was Willy, the hitchhiking grandson.

"Gosh, what took you so long, Willy?" Duane asked, giving him a big hug.

"It's hard getting a ride out of Vashti, Texas, that's what," Willy said. He shook hands with Boyd Cotton but gave his mother, his aunt, and K.K. Slater the merest nods. Willy possessed a presence all his own, and he'd had it as long as Duane could remember.

"Let's go somewhere where we can talk," he said to Duane. "We need to catch up, you and I."

"Yep, we do," Duane said, rising. "Nice to meet you, Ms. Slater. Good luck with the rhinos and the locals."

K.K. Slater said nothing, as Willy and his grandfather went out the door.

"I<small>F YOU'VE SEEN</small> one rich lady—especially one Texas rich lady—you've seen them all," Willy said. They were at Duane's house and Willy was chowing down on a bowl of Cheerios, not very substantial fare for one who had hitched from Dallas, but more or less all there was in Duane's meager larder.

"I could go get some steaks," Duane offered.

"I'm not a vegetarian but I don't think I could trust any steak sold in Thalia," Willy said.

"That's probably a sound principle," Duane admitted.

"Was that tall woman the one who's saving the rhinos?" Willy asked.

"That's the one," Duane said. "Your mother and your aunt are on her board."

"Yeah but they're so desperate for attention they'll be on any dopey board," Willy said.

"Maybe you should be on it?" Duane suggested. "Most boards could profit from a little effort from you."

"I'm too busy thinking," Willy said.

"About what?"

"Oh, the nature of reality, I guess," Willy said. "It's a large subject.

"I'm thinking of going to Norway," he added. "That's where Wittgenstein went, when he really needed to think. All I need is a table, a chair, a cot and some light."

Willy was flushed a little, with the excitement of it all.

"I know where there's an empty cabin a lot closer than Norway," Duane mentioned.

"You mean your old cabin?" Willy asked.

Duane nodded. "It might need a little patching up, but it's yours whenever you want it."

Willy considered the notion.

"Norway's cold," he said. "I don't do too well with cold. Maybe I *will* try the cabin, if you really meant it. It's pretty hard to think around Mom and her bracelets.

"I'm hungry," he added. "Is there safe food anywhere around here?"

"Seymour," Duane said. "About forty miles. I try to eat a steak there every time I come home."

"I wonder if the cold was important to Wittgenstein," Willy said. "Maybe it made thinking seem more pure."

"I wouldn't know about that," Duane admitted.

"Okay, off to Seymour," Willy said.

17

FOR MOST OF the drive to Seymour, Willy was on his cell phone, talking to his girlfriend. The steak, when they got to the little café in Seymour, was as good as ever—so good that they both had two. Willy had the twenty-four-ounce T-bone.

On the way back to Thalia they passed the North Gate. Duane honked but nobody waved.

Willy's cell phone rang again—Willy asked Duane if it was okay to answer it and Duane nodded.

"It's my teacher," Willy said. "I can't imagine why he's calling."

Willy, who had been comatose from all the steak, suddenly sat up straighter and looked stunned.

"I *did!*" he said. "For real? This is not a joke?"

Duane could tell from his voice that Willy was really excited.

"Oh my God, Dr. Jones—this is just the greatest!" Willy said.

Duane didn't know what his grandson was excited about, but he did know that the radiance that had suddenly come into his face was the radiance of success—it was the sort of radiance that came into Bobby Lee's face when he caught the big bass.

If there were prizes to win Willy usually won them, but at the moment it seemed to Duane that he had carried off a really *big* prize.

"I'm going to be a Rhodes Scholar, isn't that great!" Willy said, when he hung up.

Duane was not sure what a Rhodes Scholar actually did, though he remembered that President Clinton had been one.

"It's great if you say so," Duane said. "You look pretty happy."

"It means I get to go to England and study at Oxford for two years. I can study philosophy right there where Wittgenstein taught."

"You sure seem to put a lot of stock in this fellow Wittgenstein," Duane said.

"I do—he was so great," Willy said. "And my teacher Dr. Jones is great too."

"I bet your mama is going to be real happy when she hears this," Duane said.

Willy considered that statement for a moment.

"It's hard to say about Mom—real hard to say," he told his grandfather.

"But you know what, Grandpa? If she doesn't like it it's her problem—I'm Oxford-bound.

"That's her problem," he said again.

18

ONCE BACK AT the house, Willy disappeared into his old bedroom to tell his girlfriend the great news.

Duane called Honor Carmichael to tell *her* Willy's great news, but Honor was traveling and he only got her message machine. He would have called Annie, his wife, but she was still traveling and he wasn't exactly sure what time zone she might be in. Annie never liked being awakened and Duane decided not to take that chance.

In the past year or so he had come to like vodka. Annie's father, Cecil Cameron, on the only time he and Duane had met, spent a long time explaining to Duane how to make a vodka martini. It was the one piece of information Cecil Cameron had chosen to pass on to his son-in-law.

Duane made himself one and also made Willy one, in celebration of his prize—of course Willy might be on the phone for hours, so his celebration might have to be postponed.

While Duane was idly watching Letterman the phone rang: it was Annie.

"I was afraid you wouldn't be up," Annie said. From the tone of her voice Duane knew that something was wrong.

"I wouldn't be except that Willy's here and he just learned that he won a Rhodes Scholarship—he's burning up the wires, telling his friends."

"Congratulate him for me when you see him," Annie said. "It's not surprising that he won a Rhodes. Willy's the one real winner in your family. Tell him I'm very proud of him."

"I'll do it, where are you?" he asked—from the choked way she was speaking he knew something was really wrong.

"Munich, but it's irrelevant," Annie said. "I've fallen in love with a Frenchman and I'm going to live with him now."

"I see," Duane said, though he knew it was an inadequate thing to say, given the gravity of the message he was receiving.

There was a silence on the line.

"Duane, I know this is terrible but it is what it is," Annie said. "I feel too guilty to face you. Let's just let the lawyers handle it, okay?"

She waited, as he sat silent.

"Handle what?" he asked, before he realized what Annie meant.

"Our divorce—I'd like it if we could just break clean," she said.

"I guess we can try," he said.

"Thanks, Duane," Annie said as she hung up.

DUANE TURNED OFF Letterman. He considered making a pitcher of vodka martinis and decided against it. He couldn't avoid being sad—or, for the moment at least, shocked—but he could avoid being drunk, and he did avoid it. He sat on the couch, in the darkness, not weeping or anything—just feeling sort of blank. Annie had fallen in love with a Frenchman, and that was that. She wasn't going, she was already gone. Let the lawyers do it, and, soon enough, the lawyers would.

When Willy came in, still flushed from his triumph, the first thing he told Duane was that he would need to take a rain check on the cabin, since he'd be living in Oxford, England, soon.

"It's the perfect cabin, though," Willy said. "I might stay there for a while when I come back."

"I may move into it myself, while you're gone," Duane said. "Annie just called from Munich to say she wanted a divorce."

"Uh-oh," Willy said. "I guess I should have warned you about her."

Duane was surprised.

"How would you have known to warn me?" he asked.

"I grew up in the most rich-rich cul-de-sac in Dallas," Willy said. "It's a good place to learn about rich girls."

After that they watched a little TV.

WILLY SEEMED TO realize that all he could do for his grandfather was be there. In a while he went to bed. Duane continued to sit on the couch, and continued to feel blank. An observer might have felt that he was letting the news soak in, but the observer would have been wrong. Annie's decision soaked in immediately, perhaps because, deep down, he had been expecting it all along. In a way that was hard to put his finger on, she had never been there anyway—not really, not at the deepest level.

His first wife, Karla, even when she was not speaking to him, was nevertheless *there*, in a way that Annie Cameron had never been. Had the lack been his or hers? Was Annie, perhaps, just unable to really *be* there, as Karla had been?

If so the Frenchman she was currently in love with would someday get the kind of call that he had just got.

Around two A.M. Duane stretched out on the big, comfortable couch and attempted to doze, but could not drop off. He finally dozed, but not for long. At dawn he got up and made coffee. In time Willy came down looking fresh and managed to find a quart of orange juice in the fridge, all of which he drank. Then he was ready to go.

"I could have someone drive you back to Dallas," Duane said, but Willy politely rejected the offer.

"I'll just hitchhike," he said. "I'm good at it."

They hugged and Willy left, with nothing but a Wittgenstein book in his pocket. Duane watched him go. When he came to the highway, which was only two blocks from Duane's house, a truck with a welding rig on it stopped for him immediately. Willy waved at his grandfather and then was gone.

Willy had not said another word about Annie Cameron. The fact that Duane had a grandson who probably knew more about women than he did was a little disconcerting. His involvement with women stretched all the way back to his high school crush on the beauty queen and actress Jacy Farrell, and encompassed Karla, Jenny Marlow, cranky old Ruth Popper, and Honor Carmichael. And then Annie. He had nine grandchildren, of whom Willy was obviously the best and the brightest. Had he managed to do all this while remaining ignorant of some basic attributes of the human female?

It was a thought to ponder and, Duane soon concluded, he didn't have much to do but ponder it.

A FTER A MONTH of nights on their high perch on the Rhino Ranch, Bobby Lee and Boyd began to discover a few things they had in common, one being a fondness for whiskey. Their nocturnal duties had so far been light to the point of tedium. So far the most noteworthy action occurred when the old rhino they called Double Aught wanted to scratch his butt on the pipes that supported their tower. This produced a moment or two of mutual anxiety, but Double Aught wandered off and the tower didn't fall.

"Think he could knock this tower over if he really wanted to?" Bobby Lee asked.

"Yes," Boyd said, reaching for the bottle of Johnnie Walker Black Label they were sharing.

"What are we going to do?" Bobby Lee asked. "It's like waiting for goddamn Moby-Dick to rise."

Soon they ran out of scotch and found that they had nothing left but vodka. Boyd took the bottle but could not read the label.

"Where'd this come from?" he asked.

Before Bobby Lee could answer, Double Aught snorted.

Bobby Lee and Boyd looked around—in a minute they spotted a dim, dusk-hidden figure walking toward them on the dirt road that led north, into meth dealer land.

"It's Duane," Bobby Lee said. "Look at him. He's walking again, like he used to back when he was losing his mind."

Boyd remembered that Duane had parked his pickup for a while and walked everywhere, but, at the time, he had not known Duane well enough to know much about the state of his mind.

"I guess he's headed for that old cabin he used to live in," Bobby Lee said.

"I don't know where he's headed but it would be better if he doesn't stir up Double Aught," Boyd said.

Double Aught was still close enough to the tower for both of them to see that the old bull had pricked up his ears.

"What the hell are you doing, you fool!" Bobby Lee yelled, when Duane was in hearing distance. "You might spook this old rhino and if you do he might knock this tower over."

Double Aught, though, after his first snort, did not seem spooked.

"That would be your problem, not mine," Duane pointed out.

Boyd Cotton kept his eye on the rhino, who no longer seemed spooked. In his opinion Bobby Lee's yelling had more of a negative effect than Duane Moore's walking. He tried a mouthful of the vodka but spat it out. If Bobby Lee was feeling jangled it might be because of the vodka, rather than the rhino.

"I'm in the mood for a night in my cabin," Duane said. "I'll see you boys tomorrow."

He walked on along the darkened road. When he had gone about half a mile beyond the tower he became aware of a presence nearby—and it was a large presence.

The moon was full, and had just risen. It cast a bright glow over the mesquite flats around him.

The presence, as he had suspected, was Double Aught. "Howdy," Duane said, and kept walking, with Double Aught, across the road, keeping roughly abreast.

When Duane turned onto his property he saw that Double Aught was just standing there, watching.

"Thanks for the company," Duane said.

That night he slept well.

While cooking himself some bacon and eggs the next morning, he remembered that a rhino called Double Aught had accompanied him home.

He left his cooking for a moment to step outside and have a look around. The rhino Double Aught was nowhere to be seen.

A FEW NIGHTS LATER trouble came to the Rhino Ranch. Two good old boys from Durango, Colorado, were driving through on their way to the Gulf, where they had high-paying jobs on an offshore drilling rig.

As they neared Thalia they saw a rhinoceros standing by the road. Both had their deer rifles in the pickup—they quickly loaded up and shot the rhino dead. One of them remembered that rhino horns were supposed to be valuable, so they hurried over to one of the Wal-Marts in Wichita Falls and bought a chain saw. They hurried back to the site of the kill and proceeded to saw off the horn.

Alert on their tower, Bobby Lee and Boyd heard the sound of the saw. They had heard the shot too but supposed it was just somebody shooting a coyote, or poaching a deer. They at once called in all the law enforcement they could locate, got their rifles and soon apprehended the two Coloradans as they were preparing to drive on to the Gulf. The bloody rhino horn was in the back of the pickup, as well as the new chain saw. The two men, whose names were Lonnie and Damon, were highly indignant at being rudely addressed by an old cowboy and his skinny sidekick, both of whom were armed with more powerful rifles than either of them possessed.

"Hell, it's a free country, ain't it?" Lonnie said. "Who says there's a law against killing a damn rhino?"

"We say it," Boyd replied, in a tone that took the two poachers aback. "That was Aught Six you killed. He was our youngest bull, and he's just been here three weeks."

"I don't care how long he's been here," Damon said. "Who's gonna miss a chance to shoot a rhino?"

But soon an impressive number of police cars, patrol cars, Game and

Fish cars began to clog the country road. Lonnie and Damon were soon in handcuffs; they had been informed, to their shock, that they could be facing serious jail time. Offshore riches were not likely to be theirs, anytime soon.

And the gene pool for the African black rhino was one bull the less.

23

THE FUROR OVER the death of the young rhino, one of the few animals upon which the hope for the species depended, was not merely local, or statewide, or national: it was global. Not since two German hunters gunned down the most famous and most photographed elephant in Africa had there been such worldwide outrage.

Though the actual shooter—Lonnie—had been a Coloradan, blame for the death nevertheless stuck to Texas. A new shipment of sixteen black rhinos were due in this very week; fears for their safety filled the correspondence pages of newspapers around the world.

Boyd Cotton and Bobby Lee were briefly national heroes for having boldly detained the merciless killers—now just two miserable roughnecks with no job prospects and big legal bills.

Duane, a skeptic about rhino removal from the first, drove back to Arizona mainly to avoid the press that descended on Thalia. No one had been in the house in Patagonia, as far as he could tell. The only thing there that he really wanted was a little 28-gauge shotgun he had bought several years back and sometimes hunted with.

His pet quail were gone, though he saw a few of their cousins scuttling around the property. The loss of the quail made him sad. On a whim he drove to Ruidoso, New Mexico, where there was a pretty good racetrack. He watched the horses run until dead rhino stories began to disappear from the newspapers, at which point he drove on back to Thalia.

His cell phone, which he didn't really like, had been left in Texas, but he had taken care to leave his message machine on. He was hoping there were no calls from Annie—hearing her voice would have been difficult, just then.

There were no calls from Annie, but three from Honor Carmichael, the last one a little bit testy. Honor did not like it when she wasn't called back.

"Let me guess—Little Orphan Annie left you," Honor said, when he finally caught up with her. She and her companion had been on a Scandinavian cruise.

"How'd you know?" he asked.

"Someone I know saw her and her new guy going through customs at Kennedy," Honor said. "It's a small world, as I've pointed out to you before."

Duane didn't ask about the new guy, and Honor didn't mention him again.

"The good news is that Willy got a Rhodes Scholarship," he added.

"That *is* good news," Honor said. "It's also handy for changing the subject."

"I don't really know what to say about the subject," Duane admitted. "Annie called from Munich and said she had a new beau, and wanted a divorce. She said we should just let the lawyers handle it."

"Yes, that would be the Cameron way," Honor said. "Cold but efficient—no fuss, no bother. Why struggle with the messy details when the world is full of lawyers who will do it for you?"

"I moved back into my cabin," Duane said. "When I'm in the big house I feel like I'm just rattling around."

"You do seem sort of like you and that cabin are a fit," she said.

"Besides that I've made a friend," he said. "A rhino friend. He's about my age, I guess—they call him Double Aught."

Honor was silent for a moment.

"Good lord," she said. "How does a rhino manifest his friendship?"

"One night he walked me home," Duane said.

"I thought those rhinos were there to breed other rhinos," Honor said.

"Maybe he's like me—a little old for the girls," he said.

"That's nonsense," Honor said. "You aren't too old for the girls. What about K.K. Slater?"

"I met her once—what about her?"

"Has she made any moves?"

"I think she likes Boyd Cotton," Duane said. "They both like horses, for one thing."

Then he told her about the rednecks shooting Aught Six, and all the furor that caused.

"It might be that the rhinos are no safer in Texas than they are in Africa," Honor said.

"You hit the nail right on the head," Duane said. "You think I'll ever see Annie again?"

"I certainly hope not," Honor said.

25

BOYD AND BOBBY LEE had spent some troubled nights on the platform by the North Gate, during which they had done a pretty thorough survey of the whiskeys available at the local liquor store. Besides the Johnnie Walker they sampled Dewar's, Cutty Sark, Wild Turkey and many other popular beverages. Only vodka was tacitly scratched off the list. Bobby Lee couldn't handle it, for some reason.

The ease with which young Aught Six had been killed weighed on their consciences. The fact was that most of the vast acreage they were responsible for was bordered by narrow, sparsely traveled country roads, and most of the locals who did travel them had rifles in their pickups, and most of the drivers were tempted by large targets. Lonnie and Damon had already established that fact.

"What the hell are we going to do, Boyd?" Bobby Lee asked.

"When I took this job I thought there soon would be ten towers spread about the property," Boyd said. "So far I only count one, and that's ours. And one ain't enough."

"I think we ought to call the boss lady and stress that it's urgent that we get more help."

"Well, I'd be reluctant to do that," Boyd said.

"Why not? She likes you," Bobby Lee asked. "She spent half a day with you and never said ten words to me."

"I could call her but right now I prefer to get drunk," Boyd said.

"K.K. might be at the beauty parlor," he added. "I wouldn't want to interrupt her."

"Can you shoot when you're drunk?" Bobby Lee inquired.

"I can shoot but I can't claim I hit much shooting while under the influence," Boyd said. "Hell, I can't even rope when I'm drunk now, and I used to be able to rope in pretty much any condition. Not no more."

"I think that if any more rhinos get shot on our watch we'll get fired, and that's a dark thought for you."

"It is a dark thought," Boyd agreed. "Then you'd have to go back to spending your days getting oily, and I'd be hunting cowboying in a place where there ain't none," Boyd said.

After which, they drank.

26

THE NEXT MORNING, just after sunrise, K.K.'s white Cessna landed at the little paved airstrip that had been put in near the compound and the tower.

Since it was after sunrise Boyd and Bobby Lee had finished their shift on the tower and were off in search of breakfast, leaving Dub and Bub Hartman with the terrifying prospect of facing the boss lady, K.K. Slater, alone.

"I feel like diving off this tower right now, head first," Dub said.

"You've always been a worrier," his brother said. "The worst she can do is fire us and I'm not crazy about this job anyhow."

"Old Double Aught could knock this tower over, anytime he took a notion to," Dub remarked.

"What if K.K.'s in a bad mood?" Bub asked. He had only seen K.K. Slater once or twice, and, in any case, he had never been a very keen judge of female moods. His own girlfriend, Laurie Jenette Beaumont, mainly liked to sit on the couch, eat popcorn and watch Montel Williams. Laurie Jenette's moods seldom varied much, not even when they were doing the deed. Often, in the very midst of the deed, she would quietly drift off to sleep. At such times she was also apt to snore loudly.

Bub himself never snored while doing the deed.

As they watched, K.K. got out of the plane and came over to the tower, whose ladder she proceeded to climb.

"I asked for a car to meet me," she said, once on top. "I don't see a car. All I see is a pickup."

"That's ours," Dub said.

"Where's the Range Rover?" she asked.

"Bobby Lee just took it in for an oil change," Bub said.

There was a phone with a blinking message machine two steps behind Dub. K.K. punched the message button and heard herself addressing the tower to inform them that she was arriving at seven A.M. and would need a car. The second message said the same thing, only more emphatically.

"Could I have your pickup keys?" she asked. "I have a meeting to make."

K.K. glanced to the northwest and saw a sight that startled her. A man too far away to be recognized was walking along a dirt road, while abreast of him, one hundred yards perhaps, a massive black rhino was wandering through the mesquite, more or less keeping pace with the walker. The rhino was Double Aught.

She watched as the pair came closer.

"Son of a bitch," she said quietly to herself.

"Is this common?" she asked, turning to Bub and Dub. "Do Mr. Moore—I think that's him—and Double Aught always stroll along together like they seem to be doing now?"

Dub and Bub felt paralyzed. They knew nothing of the habits of Duane Moore, and even less about Double Aught.

"Never mind, I'll ask him myself," K.K. said.

Then she climbed down the ladder.

DUANE WAS NOT particularly surprised to find K.K. Slater waiting by the gate to the Rhino Ranch. He had heard the Cessna while it was still in the air.

Double Aught drifted over to the hay rack, where, fortunately, there was an abundance of hay.

"I didn't think people ever walked in this part of the country," K.K. said. She offered her hand and Duane shook it.

"Walking's frowned upon, I admit," Duane said. "But I have a little cabin a couple of miles from here and sometimes I feel like walking to it."

"You seem to have made a pet of Double Aught," she said. "In truth he's never been a very wild rhino. He was raised on one of those safari resorts in Kenya."

"I like him and he seems to like me but to tell you the truth I'm a little worried about him," Duane said. "What happened to Aught Six the other night could easily happen to him. The closer the old boy is to a road the more danger he's in."

"You're right, obviously—that's why I'm here," she said. Sixteen more rhinos are arriving today. You live here. How would you suggest I protect them?"

Duane had been pondering that question himself. He didn't want to wake up some morning and find Double Aught in a ditch with his horn sawed off.

"I don't know how to protect them," he said. "People around here seem to think they have a God-given right to kill big animals."

"Not just around here," K.K. said. "People in many places feel that way."

"You've got quite a bit of land here," Duane said. "If you could find some way to keep the rhinos out of sight of the roads they'd have a better chance. Not too many people would actually crawl through a fence to go after rhino."

"Not at first," K.K. said. "But eventually some will do just that—crawl through a fence to shoot at a rhino."

Duane knew she was right—human destructiveness seemed to only get worse, in relation to the value of the quarry.

He liked K.K.'s frankness—she had given the matter more thought than he had.

"Why don't you call me Duane," he said.

"Thanks, I will, Duane," K.K. Slater said.

DUANE RODE INTO Thalia with K.K. He saw that her face was lined, in the way real ranch women's faces came to be after many years in the sun and wind.

"I wish you'd indulge me just once and come to the meeting I called," she said, parking the Hartman brothers' pickup at the courthouse.

"All right," Duane said. "What kind of folks will I get to meet?"

"Well, there'll be the nonprofit world. I doubt you've spent much time in that world."

He waited.

"That means we'll hear from the Nature Conservancy, the World Wildlife Fund, a sprinkle of Game and Fish types, the state Chamber of Commerce and for kicks a Texas Ranger I invited. He's my beau, sort of."

"I think the Texas Ranger name still carries some weight," he said. "If they was to assign us a Ranger or two I think the rhinos might stand a little better chance."

"I need to eat before I tackle this crowd," K.K. said.

"There's always the Dairy Queen," he reminded her. "You already know what their chicken-frys are like."

"Let's hit it," K.K. said. "You're paying. I forgot to grab my billfold when I took off this morning."

When they reached the Dairy Queen thirty-two combines were lined up down the road in front of it; which meant that the wheat harvest was just about to get underway. The same machines would harvest their way north and be in Manitoba at summer's end.

"This place is too crowded—maybe we should run down to the next town," she said.

"Not to worry," Duane said. He nodded at Maybelle the cook—five minutes later they had their order: eggs up, sausage, grits and biscuits.

The combiners looked a little surprised when they noticed Duane and

K.K.'s food marching by, but they were excited to be starting the harvest and didn't say anything.

"This doesn't seem very democratic, dare I say," K.K. said.

"I used to be important here," Duane said. "Now my main privilege is getting my eats quick."

"Does your privilege follow you into the bedroom?" she asked.

"Nope," Duane said.

"I didn't think so," K.K. said.

29

A s THEY WERE eating a very clean state patrol car pulled in and parked near the window where they were eating.

"Who's that?" Duane asked.

K.K. smiled—she looked girlish, for a moment.

"My beau," she said. "Hondo Honda."

Duane was not sure whether she spoke seriously or in jest.

Hondo Honda got out of the car, put an immaculate Stetson on his head and took a Winchester rifle in a fringed scabbard out of the back seat.

"Does he always bring a rifle to breakfast?" Duane asked.

"Everywhere—he brings it everywhere," K.K. said.

Duane noticed that, besides the rifle, Hondo Honda also had a sizable revolver with pearl grips.

"Are you sure we're not in a movie?" he asked.

"Just don't embarrass him, Duane," she said. "He'll embarrass himself soon enough."

When Hondo Honda stepped inside, the thirty or so combiners looked at him in surprise.

"It's okay, John Wayne," one said, putting his hands up high. "Whatever we done we plead guilty to. I'd hate to be shot full of holes in a fuckin' Dairy Queen."

"Uh-oh," K.K. said. "Hondo won't tolerate rude behavior."

Hondo Honda could not hide a look of perplexity. He had showed up in Thalia at K.K.'s request and now this big stout boy in a University of Nebraska T-shirt seemed almost to be making fun of him.

While he was considering his options Boyd Cotton walked in. He had to step around Hondo to gain a clean path to Duane's table.

"'Lo, cowboy," Hondo said.

Hondo had taken off his hat, but couldn't find a place to put it.

The room relaxed.

"What's wrong with that Texas Ranger?" Boyd asked, mildly. He put his own worn Stetson on his knee.

"Nothing that isn't wrong with the majority of his kind," K.K. said.

Eventually, finding no hat rack, Hondo Honda sat down with them. He followed Boyd Cotton's example and put his fine hat on his knee.

30

"THREE YEARLING RHINOS got out last night," Boyd informed his boss. "They got out on the far west side. I brought them back but I doubt they'll stay around unless we get that tubular fencing up pretty soon.

"They're not that different from cows, they just weigh more," he added.

"Sixteen big ones are coming today," K.K. reminded him.

"All the more reason to get the good fencing started," Boyd said. His breakfast arrived unbidden, his eggs fried hard, as was the cowboy custom. They were accompanied by a double order of biscuits and gravy.

"Was there foul play in the yearlings' escape?" Hondo inquired. "I hear there's been foul play up here already—probably Mexicans behind it."

"No, it was two white men from Durango, Colorado," Boyd told him. For some reason the big Ranger rubbed him the wrong way.

"You're gonna need adequate fencing and you're going to need it quick," Duane told K.K., wondering why she had bothered to call in Hondo. Then he remembered she had said he was her beau.

"We'll get to the fencing," K.K. said. "There's been a slight hitch in our plans but I hope we can clear it up today."

But her tone had changed—from being the model of the decisive billionairess she was muted, tentative. Hondo Honda stared at her with frank adoration.

Duane paid the check and Boyd Cotton took care of the tip . . . a crumpled dollar bill.

Duane felt so strongly that something was amiss that he decided just to ask.

"K.K. is something wrong?" he asked.

"How'd you guess?" she said. "In fact something *is* wrong.

"Bad wrong," she added.

"I'm broke, that's what's wrong," she went on. "I can't even afford to buy three guys breakfast at a goddamned Dairy Queen."

Duane was stunned. She was a billionairess—the only one he had ever met. Pedigree didn't mean that much in Texas, unless it involved race horses, but K.K. was from one of the oldest families in the state.

How could she be broke?

Then he did recall that it had been said of the oilman Bunker Hunt that he was so rich he couldn't go broke if he tried.

Then he promptly went broke.

"How can you be broke?" he asked.

"My brothers, that's how," she told him, before bursting into tears.

31

K.K. CRIED HARD, but she didn't cry long.

"Would you happen to have a handkerchief in your pocket?" she asked Duane, which he did and which he happily lent her.

When her eyes cleared she looked at the cars parked at the courthouse. She shook her head, evidently annoyed by the sight of cars, most of which were not the kind of cars one found in Thalia.

"Second-tier!" she muttered, a comment that meant nothing to Duane.

"My brothers and I are battling over the Slater Trust," she said. "It's one of the largest in the world, and the income from it allows me to fund charities such as the Rhino Ranch.

"Word has leaked that my asshole brothers are trying to break the Slater Trust," she said. "This could mean Armageddon in the nonprofit world. I called this meeting to try a little damage control."

"Who'll be here?" he asked, noticing that none of the cars currently parked on the square seemed to be American-made. None of them looked like they'd be cheap, either.

"Well, Donna, from the Texas Chamber of Commerce," K.K. said. "She's probably a slightly more vulgar version of your wife. There'll be a perfectly nice wimp from the Nature Conservancy, and a distant cousin of Prince Philip who's with the World Wildlife Fund. I had hoped Boone Pickens would show up—Boone likes fights, but I think he's out of the country."

Duane felt a little swamped. Boone Pickens, and a cousin of Prince Philip, in Thalia, Texas? Had there ever been such a show?

"My father knew I was smarter than all my brothers put together, so he put me over the trust," K.K. said.

Just then a lawyerish figure stepped out of the courthouse, looked around until he spotted K.K. and then waved frantically at her.

"I guess the judge just showed up," Duane ventured.

"No judge, this is just about fund-raising," she said. "Several prominent institutions have put money into the rhino project, and, being institutions, they hedge every bet they can hedge, If it gets on the wire that my brothers are trying to break the Slater Trust, then every ecology-related charity would feel immediate frostbite."

"Why bring them here, if it's not a trial?" Duane asked.

"Because I can," K.K. said. "I want to get them on unfamiliar ground. Making them uncomfortable never hurts."

Duane had the feeling that he was on unfamiliar ground himself, despite the fact that he was in his hometown.

"Plus we're getting sixteen more rhinos this afternoon," she said. "That would provide lots of photo ops, which would give them nice snaps to take back to their boards."

Just then Boyd Cotton drove up and parked beside them. Boyd had changed into a clean blue work shirt, and was wearing his rodeo boots, a fact Duane noticed when they all got out of their vehicles.

A moment later a white Lexus drew up and parked beyond Boyd. It was Dickie Moore, in a suit that matched his car.

"What a handsome son you have," K.K. said. "Besides which he doesn't miss much."

As they headed up the sidewalk to the courthouse they saw Hondo Honda, minus his rifle for once, walking ahead of them.

"My Ranger," K.K. said, and smiled.

A moment later, not wishing to be upstaged by Boyd, Bobby Lee emerged from his Toyota pickup. He wore a Rhino Enterprises dozer cap and Levi's so new they practically stood alone.

"If there's any excitement happening I want to be in on it," he said. "I *was* the first local employee of Rhino Enterprises—beat Boyd out by an hour."

K.K. laughed; she liked Bobby Lee, though it was a different liking from what she felt for Boyd Cotton.

"If we count that Texas Ranger we're a force of six," Bobby Lee said. "One more and we could call ourselves the Magnificent Seven."

"Double Aught should be number seven," Duane said. "If the charity folks get cranky we could have him stomp on their cars or something."

There was a moment of silence. Then they all went in.

DONNA L'ENGLE, head fieldworker for the Texas Chamber of Commerce, *was* rather Annie-like—skinny, good-looking, short brown hair and, at the moment, pissed off.

"Who's this mob?" she asked, as the bunch of them trooped in. They were in an old shabby courtroom that the county had no money to fix up. There was no podium or judge's bench, just three bare tables and some chairs.

Hondo Honda, unasked, strolled to the front of the room and stood there stiffly, doing a good imitation of a bailiff.

A young man with long blond hair, a fringed leather jacket and snakeskin boots smiled when he saw Hondo.

"What are you doing here, Hondo?" he asked. "Concerned as we all are about the situation I'm not sure we needed to call out the Rangers."

"Fuck off, Rick," K.K. said. "I asked him to come."

"Rick and I work out of Fort Worth," Donna said, quite obviously still pissed off. "Hugo has offices in Dallas, thirty miles away. You were in Fort Worth last night yourself, K.K. So why did we have to drag ourselves up here?"

"I thought you might want to get your pictures taken with the sixteen new rhinos we're getting any minute now," K.K. said. "After all, your money helped bring them here."

A tall man in a dark suit walked in.

K.K. smiled. "Thanks for coming, Hugo," she said.

"Thank us all for coming," Donna L'Engle said. "Who are the three gentlemen I don't know?"

"My crew," K.K. said. "I thought while we were here we might thrash out the little tizzy Donna has been having over the Slater Trust."

"*Little* tizzy?" Donna said.

"If put in perspective, yes, Donna," K.K. said. "Families quarrel. My own mother tried for twenty years to break that trust and she failed. My brothers are at most half as smart as my mother, and I would bet the Hope Diamond that they fail too."

"You don't own the Hope Diamond," Rick said.

"I know—that's why I'd bet it," she said. Then she smiled.

"These legal challenges can take years, K.K.—you just said that yourself," Donna pointed out. "Who's going to fund Rhino Enterprises while this little family quarrel works its way through the courts?"

"No problem, we will, ma'am," Dickie said, startling everyone.

"Who's *we*?" Donna asked.

"Moore Drilling," Dickie said. "We're your neighbors from just across the road."

Except for a sneeze from Bobby Lee there was dead silence in the room.

"Not to be rude, sir, but do you know how much money this enterprise absorbs?" Donna asked.

"I do, and we have it with room to spare," Dickie said.

To everyone's surprise, Hondo Honda, up to then as stationary as a wooden Indian, suddenly grabbed his hat and went racing toward the door.

"Forgot to lock my car, somebody might steal my rifle," he announced as he disappeared.

"Odd fellow, that," the tall man named Hugo said. It proved to be his only comment on the proceedings at hand.

33

DICKIE MOORE'S SUDDEN intervention, plus Hondo Honda's strange dash, left the room momentarily stunned, except for the tall, inscrutable Hugo, who showed neither interest nor concern.

"If you knew you had a patron why didn't you just call us and tell us, K.K.?" Donna asked.

"Reasons of my own, darling," K.K. said.

"And stop calling me 'darling,'" Donna insisted.

"Oh, Donna, relax, we're all friends here," Rick said. He fiddled with his key ring, which was shaped like a buffalo.

"In a pig's eye," Donna said, and just as she said it Myles Vane, wearing an Australian bush hat, stepped into the room.

"Sixteen rhinos at your pleasure," he said. "We'll be unloading in about half an hour. The TV trucks are all in place and there's a fair sprinkling of press."

"Thanks, Myles," K.K. said, standing up. "Let's go, folks. Another great day for the black rhino, and a pretty good day for Texas, for that matter."

Mention of photo ops seemed to heal all wounds. Donna L'Engle dashed off to the ladies' to freshen her makeup, and Rick, whose last name Duane didn't know, combed his hair carefully before putting on his hat, which was leather, like his coat.

Outside the courthouse Hondo Honda was showing his rifle and scabbard to two old-timers on the spit and whittle bench. Hondo seemed to enjoy being a Texas Ranger, now that his rifle was secure.

"You can go along, sweetie, if you want to," K.K. said.

Hondo beamed.

"You were a big help," K.K. added. Hondo beamed some more before humbly getting behind the wheel. He took off his hat, put it on the seat beside him and drove away.

"Sweetie? You called that asshole sweetie?" Donna said. "Why?"

"Because I adore him," K.K. said.

34

DUANE WALKED OVER and had a word with his son, who was chatting away with Donna L'Engle. Duane had plenty of faith in his son's judgment but he was still a little surprised by what had occurred. However, Dickie and Donna seemed to have it off because Donna hopped in the Lexus.

"I make friends quick," Dickie said to his father, with a grin.

"You do," Duane said. "And you also seem to have gotten us in the rhino business quick."

"That's because I'm betting on K.K.," Dickie said. "K.K. don't lose."

Dickie hopped into his Lexus, made a big U-turn and headed for the Rhino Ranch.

Boyd and Bobby Lee followed the Lexus, in their respective cars. Duane noticed that K.K. and the tall, enigmatic Hugo were in animated conversation, in a language that Duane was pretty sure was French.

As Duane approached, the two kissed one another on both cheeks. Hugo nodded to Duane and then folded himself into a silver Jaguar, which smoothly purred away, toward the photo op.

"That was French, wasn't it?" he asked.

"It wouldn't be to a Frenchman, but of course I had my years in Paris. Hugo and I resort to it when we don't want anyone else to know what we're saying."

She started to get into the Hartman twins' battered pickup, but noticed that Duane held back.

"What? You're not interested in our new babies?"

"I'll be by," Duane said. "I just feel like walking."

"Okay. I know you were enjoying a hike when I dragged you into this," K.K. said. "Anything wrong?"

"What do the two Ks stand for?" he asked.

"Kittie Kay—that will give you some idea of how evil my mother was," she said.

They pondered that a moment, then she put the pickup in gear.

"Enjoy your walk," she said, and drove away.

35

Not eager to join the crowd of press, local gawkers, rhino handlers and whatever flotsam drove up on the road, Duane walked over to his house and slipped into the hot tub for a while.

He kept the hot tub set at 106 degrees, which was hotter than most people liked it, but which was just right to cook Duane into a state of relaxation.

Just before the breakup Annie had given him some fancy walking shoes with unnecessarily long strings. He had to tie them in triple knots to keep from stepping on the ends, and usually he stepped on the ends anyway. He was a mind to throw the irritating shoes away, but held back for the moment. He was ninety-nine percent certain that Annie Cameron was out of his life forever, but one percent was one percent; if she should show up he didn't want to have to tell her he'd thrown her final gift away.

As he passed Jenny Marlow's house she stuck her head out the door and waved.

"They're unloading the rhinos right now—I can watch it on TV and not run the risk of getting trampled," Jenny said. "You can come in and watch if you want to."

"Thanks, but if I don't walk I've got nothing to do," he told her.

"I can remember when you worked harder than anyone in town," Jenny said. "That boy of yours sure looks good in a suit.

"I wonder where he gets that from?" she asked. "I don't ever remember seeing you in a suit, long as I've known you."

"I wore a suit to Ruth Popper's funeral," Duane said. "And I wore a suit to my most recent wedding, although I never got around to putting on the tie.

"Annie said a tie made me look like a social climber," he added. "Don't you think that's kind of an odd thing for a bride to say to her groom?"

Jenny grinned.

"You want to know what I told Lester when we got married—I told him to wash his dick. I was real prudish in those days."

"On that cheery note I'm leaving," Duane said.

36

WHEN HE REACHED the edge of town he looked up the road and saw that the Rhino Ranch was, for the moment, a mob scene. Pickups with horse trailers and oilfield vehicles filled the shoulders of the road on both sides.

Of course that was normal. How many chances did roughnecks, cowboys and snowbirds get to see a group of African black rhinos get unloaded?

As he got closer to the scene the size of the crowd alarmed him even more. Why had Hondo Honda left just when there was a real crowd control crisis—just the kind of crisis Rangers were supposed to be good at?

For no clear reason, Duane found himself growing ever more anxious. The rhino handlers were professionals—they had transported many large animals and knew what to do.

And, in any case, what was happening was none of his business. He had no responsibility at the moment at all. He could just circle the big spectacle, go to his cabin, and rest. But something was shaking him up, and he needed to figure out what it was and what it meant.

He could see his own son, in his brilliant white suit, chatting happily with Donna L'Engle—Rick Rice, from the Nature Conservancy, had joined them. K.K. was listening soberly to the mayor of Thalia; nearby was a pudgy woman that Duane thought might be the lieutenant governor. Bobby Lee was chatting with one of the local newscasters—when he spread his hands Duane deduced that he was probably talking about his fish.

Several people saw him and waved—Duane politely waved back, but did not join the crowd. He circled the unloading and the celebration and went on to his cabin. Since his heart surgery he had acquired a kind of crowd-phobia—perhaps that had caused him to skirt the celebration.

When he was a mile or two beyond the North Gate he began to relax.

He heard the popping of brush behind him and looked around to see Double Aught following him, just as he had the other night.

When Duane stopped, so did the rhino.

"Now this is foolish," Duane said. "You ought to be back with your new friends, getting your picture taken. You might get yourself a nice frisky girlfriend if you sniff around a little."

Double Aught ignored this advice, but he did investigate a patch of sunflowers growing near the bar ditch. Not finding the sunflowers to his liking, he turned his attention to a small yucca plant—with better results.

"You don't see that many yucca in this country now," Duane said. "There's plenty of it farther west."

Double Aught rumbled.

Duane took that for an answer and strolled on home.

37

Duane took a nap and woke up hungry. The only food in the house was a can of tomato soup, which he heated and ate. He would have liked some crackers but unfortunately had none. The Asia Wonder Deli was a blazing six miles away. He usually kept a cheap bicycle at the cabin for just such emergencies, but his last one had been stolen, by some meth dealers likely.

He had hoped Dickie would swing by, to explain why Moore Drilling was suddenly expanding into the rhino import business—but Dickie did not swing by.

One thing Duane did know was that Dickie was thoroughly profit-driven. If he linked Moore Drilling to Rhino Enterprises it was because he expected to get something out of it: profit, publicity, new investors, something.

While they were living in Arizona Annie had given him a book called *Desert Solitaire*. Its author, Edward Abbey, seemed to be a sort of local hero. Duane was not sure why this was so, but, every now and then, he read a few pages at random, and usually enjoyed what he read.

The one can of soup did not make him much less hungry—he took the Abbey book out under his favorite shade tree and read a few pages. Across the mesquite flats he could still see the numerous cars and pickups parked by the Rhino Ranch. He dozed a little and was awakened by the sound of a pickup coming up the road. From the rattle he knew it must be the Hartman boys' pickup, but why was it coming up this road. From the other side of the road, Double Aught watched the pickup too. Evidently he didn't like the sound, because he trotted off to the west.

The pickup stopped at the wire gate, and K.K. got out to open it. Then she saw Duane, sitting under his shade tree with his book.

From the west Double Aught was watching them both—though not in a hostile way.

"I don't mean to interrupt your reading, but would you take me to lunch?"

"Be glad to," Duane said. "I'm pretty near starving myself."

THE LINE AT the Asia Wonder Deli was long, but K.K. insisted that they observe the democratic niceties, and stand in it. There were two tiny tables inside the deli, one of which they eventually captured. Sitting at a table meant that you didn't have to juggle your food, but what it didn't provide was privacy. The line that they had stood in, still long, was only a foot away.

That didn't matter much, because the two of them were too hungry to talk. Mike and Tommy clucked in amazement at the amount of barbecued pork K.K. tucked away.

"Ever serve barbecue goat?" she asked the two of them, as Duane paid the check.

"Goat? Baby goat—I have for pet," Tommy said.

"You forget about that when you're eating them," K.K. said. "That's two meals you've bought me today, Duane."

"I'm not usually this extravagant," he said.

K.K. looked skeptical.

"I think you're as extravagant as the woman you're feting wants you to be," she said.

"Which is a way of saying I think you're a pushover—at least you are if you like the woman you're with," she said.

Duane reflected on that judgment as they wound their way back along the dusty road. When he and Karla first married they were poor and had to watch their money, though not to any extreme degree. But once the boom came and they became rich, watching their money meant mainly watching it go out.

Years and decades passed and it was still going out, through the spigots of his daughters and their kids—Willy being the exception to the spigot rule.

"Now that I'm back to batching there may not be too many more opportunities for me to be extravagant," he said.

"Were you surprised when I said I was broke this morning?" she asked.

"Are you broke?" he asked.

"Only until I get back to Fort Worth," she said. "When I heard my brothers were trying to break the Slater Trust I left so quickly that I didn't grab a wallet or a checkbook. Mostly I don't carry money myself—I have a person named Roland who usually travels with me, and Roland carries the money, but his wife is due to have a baby about now, so I left him in South Texas.

"I'm getting behind with you, though," she said. "You're two meals up on me."

When they got back to the gate that led to his cabin Duane wondered if he should ask her in and then did ask her in.

"It's not much but I like it," he said.

K.K. took a quick look inside and came out.

"It's what we call a line cabin, on our ranch," she said. "We have more than three hundred thousand acres under one fence—that's a lot of line to ride. The vaqueros need someplace they can bunk for the night. We have about twenty of these little shacks.

"I can see how it suits you," K.K. said. "It wouldn't surprise me if you lived out your life here—in which case why won't you sell me your big house in town?"

"Because Willy likes the big house," he said.

K.K. smiled. "Okay, I can take that as a clincher. If I'm around here much I might just have to build myself a house."

"There's a little hotel that's for sale, I understand," Duane said. "It's got about ten rooms. You could probably make it into some kind of house, if you wanted to."

"That's a thought," she said.

When she left Duane closed the gate behind her. The pickup threw up a cloud of whitish dust as K.K. Slater drove along the narrow country road.

39

OBBY LEE AND BOYD were drinking straight bourbon atop their tower at the North Gate of the Rhino Ranch. A fine western sunset inflamed the distant horizon. Three rhinos stood a hundred yards away, flecked with golden light.

Bobby Lee kept looking up the dirt road to the north, hoping to see Duane coming. Duane and K.K. had spent a good part of the afternoon together, a fact which should have produced news, by now. But it hadn't.

"Maybe there ain't no news," Boyd suggested.

"Sure there is—why wouldn't there be?" Bobby Lee said. "She's a billionairess. Everything she does is news."

"Probably she's got the hots for Duane," he said. "It wouldn't hurt him to come and tell us about it."

"She doesn't have the hots for Duane," Boyd said. "She's got too much on her mind."

Bobby Lee thought Boyd's reasoning was strange, to say the least.

"I've never yet had so much on my mind that I couldn't get the hots," he said.

"You're the exception that proves the rule," Boyd said.

"What rule?"

"No rule. I was just hoping you'd shut up so I could enjoy the sunset," Boyd told him.

Bobby Lee continued to look up the road, but he was losing hope.

The sun-flecked rhinos had wandered off.

Boyd Cotton continued to drink.

DUANE PAID ONE of his rare visits to the offices of Moore Drilling, in Wichita Falls. He had had to hitchhike in, but since most of the pickups that passed belonged to his crew it didn't prove hard to get a ride.

Dickie was in jeans and a denim work shirt. A small blizzard of e-mails flowed in from various computers—it was a far cry from the day when Moore Drilling just had one typewriter, and that jealously guarded by Ruth Popper.

Dickie looked a little frazzled, Duane thought.

"I wish Annie hadn't run off from us," Dickie said. "Fickle or not she's the only one who can keep up with the flow of e-mails on a busy day."

"Is she fired, then?"

"Well, she's not fired—but she's not here, either, and here is where the e-mails are."

"It's funny K.K. came up here broke," Duane said.

"No, it's normal," Dickie said. "Her kind of rich rarely carry money. K.K. has a little handler named Roland, who normally carries her money."

"I still kind of like to carry my own money, when I have any," Duane said. Below them he saw a very pretty secretary strolling across the parking lot on her way to work.

"That's our new girl, Casey Kincaid," Dickie said. "Casey always looks as if she's just been fucked, and she probably has just been fucked."

"But not by me," Dickie said, seeing his father raise his eyebrow. "I think I know enough now to keep it out of the office."

"So what's your real feeling about Rhino Enterprises, which I guess you're eager to invest in, at least you were yesterday," Duane said.

"I was and I am—it could be a tourist gold mine," Dickie said. "We need to sort of inch it away from the nonprofits, though. It'll take them another year just to authorize that fencing, and we need that good pipe fencing done right away.

"There's thirty-nine rhinos now, and nothing but that crappy little barbed wire fencing to keep them in—not good."

"That's been worrying me too," Duane said. "If somebody don't get that fence up there will be be rhinos turning up all over the West, pretty soon. Or one will charge a school bus and there'll be hell to pay."

"Right," Dickie said. "I think there's some kind of contract with a fencing company out of Dallas, but so far, other than bringing the pipes, they haven't done squat."

"Maybe we should start a little fencing company ourselves," Duane suggested. "I could run it—it would give me something to do that I understand."

"That's not a bad idea—only I wouldn't want you to do the heavy work."

"Bulldozers and heavy diggers and cranes and winches do the heavy work now," Duane reminded Dickie. "I'd just sit in the cool and supervise."

"That's not a bad idea," Dickie said.

But his mind was on Casey Kincaid, who was idly reading e-mails. She still looked as if she'd just been fucked.

"Let's think about taking over the fencing, anyway," Duane said. "And if Casey ain't doing anything crucial maybe she could run me home."

"I bet she could," Dickie said. "Casey's never doing anything important, except reminding me that I'm male.

"But you're male too," he added.

"Only off and on," Duane said.

41

N O SOONER WERE they in the company pickup than Casey offered
Duane a piece of gum—in fact, several pieces of gum. She was wearing plenty of perfume, so much, in fact, that he had to lower his window a bit. The perfume was so strong that he was afraid it might give him a sore throat. This had happened once or twice when he was at Dillard's or somewhere, shopping for perfume for Karla or Annie.

"I don't know what I'd do if I couldn't chew gum," Casey informed him.

Casey leaned over the wheel of the pickup, chewing so vigorously that it caused her young breasts to move a little as she chewed.

"Do you mind that I'm promiscuous?" she asked.

Did he mind that she was promiscuous?

"I don't," Duane said. "I don't know much about you, really."

"A lot of Texans are pretty puritanical," she said. "It's the only thing I don't like about living here. I come from San Diego. The only reason I'm here is that I married an airman for a while. His dick was nearly a foot long, you know? I tried my best to get him into the porn movie business. With a dick like that he would have been a big star. But the asshole was too shy. Before I met him he'd never even fucked anyone in the butt. He was a Baptist and he said Baptists didn't do that, but of course they do. Everybody butt-fucks, wouldn't you say?"

"It's that road," Duane said, pointing to the dirt road that led through the brush to his cabin.

Casey hit the dirt road going about sixty, throwing up a huge cloud of white dust.

Duane decided to pass on the issue of butt-fucking.

"Personally I don't see any contradiction between religion and fucking," Casey said. "I mean, if God didn't make cocks and cunts, who did? And if God made them there can't be too much wrong with them?"

Uninvited, Casey began to take her shirt off while she drove. She wore a sleeveless undershirt.

"I hate scratchy old shirts," she said. "On the beach in San Diego I mainly went nude, and nobody cared, since they were mostly nude too."

"Not too much nudity around here," Duane said, feeling silly.

"I've never fucked a real old man like you," Casey said. "I'd kind of like to try it. What do you think?"

Duane shrugged and smiled. When Annie Cameron dumped him he supposed he had come to the end of his sex life. He looked at Casey again, a little more closely, and concluded that, despite her full breasts, he was in a pickup with a teenager.

"Are you of age, Casey?" he asked bluntly.

"Shit, you would ask me that, you old fart," she said, pouting a little.

When they came to his cabin she braked hard and stopped. He got out and opened the gate. Then he walked around to her side of the pickup and thanked her for bringing him home.

"You're passing on me because of two lousy months?" she said.

"I think we better hold off," Duane said, not entirely without mixed feelings. Casey was doing her best to look trashy, but she wasn't quite making it. She had a brief flare-up.

"Hey, I was fucking a guy with a foot-long dick," she said. "How long do you think it would take me to wring you out, Grandpa?"

"Oh, not long," Duane said.

Tears suddenly began to leak out of Casey's eyes.

"Why are things so hard?" she asked. "Even a simple thing like fucking gets all tangled up with laws and stuff."

"Thanks for bringing me home," Duane said.

Perhaps because of her tears Casey had not noticed his cabin. When he pointed at it she looked aghast.

"You live in *that*?" she asked. "Oh my gosh I would never want to fuck somebody who lived in *that*. You were right to turn me down, and you even did it kind of nicely, at that."

She paused, spat out her gum and quickly inserted a few fresh sticks.

"I bet you reject most girls—we probably seem dopey to you," Casey said.

"No, you don't seem dopey," he said. "My son doesn't hire dopey girls."

"Dickie, he's not into fucking, either," Casey said.

Duane didn't contradict her, though he knew that chastity wasn't Dickie's strong suit.

"I hate working—it sucks," Casey said.

"It has its downside," Duane admitted.

"Yep, and fucking doesn't, though of course you might run into a limp dick or maniac once in a while.

"Do you even have a TV?" she asked, looking at the cabin again.

"Not out here," Duane admitted. "I've got one in town."

She killed the pickup and started to walk with him toward the cabin.

"I just want to peek in," she assured him.

And she did peek in, quickly reviewing Duane's few possessions.

"Did you ever pee into anyone?" she asked. "I mean while you're fucking or after you've fucked. Urine is a very clean liquid, you know. Ever try peeing into anyone?"

"Nope."

"Do you at least have a hot tub, in town, maybe?"

"I do," he said.

"Maybe when I'm legal I'll come and visit you," Casey said. "I can give underwater BJs too."

Just then they heard a grunt, from outside the cabin.

Duane stepped around Casey and looked out. Sure enough, twenty feet away, stood Double Aught.

The great beast standing by the pickup didn't seem to worry Casey Kincaid at all.

"Oh good, it's just a rhino," she said. "Shoo, rhino."

Obediently, Double Aught turned and trotted off.

"That's the first time he crossed the road," Duane said, mainly to himself.

He was trying his best to keep the conversation off sex.

"Two months isn't very long," Casey said. "I bet you won't be so puritanical once I get you in the hot tub."

Then she got in the pickup and left.

NEWS OF CASEY KINCAID's arrival on the North Texas oil and gas scene was not slow to spread.

Reports that Duane Moore had taken her alone to his cabin, where very few people had ever been, were also not slow to spread.

Evaluations of her beauty quietly circulated.

Estimates of her age were bruited about.

Bobby Lee saw her pass through a stoplight and was so smitten that he was later given a ticket for going sixty-six in a thirty-mile zone.

"I was just trying to catch up with my boss, Duane Moore," he pleaded, but his plea fell on deaf ears.

"I think you were thinking of making cat tracks on the ceiling," the officer, whose name was Roy, said.

"The ceiling of this car," Roy added. "And you was hoping to be between the legs of that long-legged girl."

"I see you have no sympathy for the workingman," Bobby Lee said, determined to stand on his dignity.

"Girls like that one that you was chasing belong in Cancun," Roy said. "Have you ever been to Cancun?"

"I did go there once," Bobby Lee lied. "That was because my first wife won a raffle."

"I don't believe your lying ass," Roy said, and wrote the ticket, which was for just over one hundred dollars.

"Ouch," Bobby Lee said.

"I DON'T WANT HER in our house," Annie Cameron said.

The call had come out of the blue, to his cell phone, while he was sitting under his shade tree reading *Desert Solitaire*.

"Who?"

"Casey Kincaid, you know who, you son of a bitch," Annie said.

"I meant our house in Patagonia," she said. "I don't want you bringing her there."

"But Annie, that's your house—it went back to you in the divorce papers," he reminded her. "It was really your parents'. I never thought of it as mine. Anyway, I'm in Texas, at my cabin," he said. "My only other house is the big house in town."

"I couldn't even ride that far with Casey Kincaid," he went on. "Her perfume would suffocate me before we got to Abilene."

"Cheap perfume is what you get when you date sluts," she told him, in a cold tone.

"I don't date Casey or anybody, for that matter," he said. "Casey works for Dickie."

"Then he's probably fucking her," Annie said.

"Last I heard she went back to her husband," he said.

"Oh, the one with the foot-long dick? I heard about him too."

"Then you know everything I know, if not more," Duane said. "How are you otherwise?"

"Duane, let's not start," she said, and hung up.

The call had not produced one affectionate comment, a fact that made Duane sad. He sat under his shade tree all afternoon, but made little progress on *Desert Solitaire*.

Now and then he looked across the road, but his friend the rhino Double Aught was nowhere to be seen.

44

"I wish I still worked for Moore Drilling—at least I wish it sometimes," Bobby Lee said to Boyd. "If I still worked for the Moores I could find some excuse to visit the office. Then, with luck, I could look at Casey Kincaid's top, or up her skirt."

"Invent an excuse and go there anyway, if it means that much to you," Boyd suggested.

"I heard she offered to suck Dickie's cock for two thousand dollars," Bobby Lee said. "Of course that's just rumor."

"So did she?" Boyd asked, after a pause.

"Nope, said he had to refuse in order to keep down inflation," Bobby Lee said.

Far to the west six or seven rhinos were grazing. Boyd got his binoculars and looked closely, but nothing seemed to be amiss. A few white cattle egrets were scattered among the rhinos. There was a coyote trotting along one of the feed roads in the pasture, but he paid no attention to the rhinos, nor did the rhinos pay attention to him.

Boyd had resorted to the binoculars mainly because a pretense of attention would free him, for a few minutes, from having to listen to Bobby Lee. He didn't dislike Bobby Lee. He just got tired of listening to him.

"THERE'S A GIRL after me, Willy," Duane told his grandson, on the phone.

"I know—my mom is pissed off at Dickie because he hired her. She's supposed to be involved with an airman with a foot-long dick."

"Things like that are often exaggerated," Duane said.

"I haven't had sex yet, so I wouldn't know," Willy said. "Maybe I'll lose my virginity in England."

"Don't worry if you don't," Duane told him. "Sex is in your life for a long time, even if you start a little late. You'll eventually add up a lot of sex—forty or fifty years' worth."

There was a silence.

"Right now you don't believe sex could ever be boring, but it can," Duane said.

"I guess I can accept that in theory," Willy said. "But I'm a long way from being there yet. Will you come to see me when I'm in England? I'll be there for two years."

"I'll mosey over, at some point," Duane said.

"Good," Willy said.

46

"I GUESS YOU'RE SOME kind of magnet for cunty women," Honor told Duane, who was cooking sausage on the little stove in the cabin. Honor sounded mildly peeved.

"I guess news travels faster than it used to," Duane said. "E-mail, I guess."

"Yes, e-mail," Honor said. "I even have a few pictures of the divine Casey myself."

"All that happened is that she gave me a ride home from the office," he told her.

He cracked three eggs and proceeded to scramble them; he also slipped two pieces of Wonder Bread into his ancient toaster.

He was aware that both Honor and Annie, not to mention his daughters, would have scorned the breakfast, but then fortunately none of them were there.

"Nothing happened, Honor," he said. "Why Dickie hired such a little slut I don't know—but I didn't hire her and I expect her to quit anyday."

"She probably didn't mention this, but Sid Cameron, your former father-in-law, used to chase little Casey Kincaid around his yacht," Honor said. "The West Coast yachting set has known about little Casey for a long time."

"She's supposed to have an airman husband who's pretty well hung," he told her. "A foot in length has been mentioned. I always thought that big dick stuff was hooey."

"It is, for most women," Honor said. "But Casey Kincaid is a porn star—or was. In porn the requirements are a little different."

"I see," Duane said. He was anxious to get on with his breakfast. Honor no longer sounded peeved, so, after a little more chitchat, he hung up.

47

Jenny marlow did not win her battle with the Big C. Once she concluded that the battle was lost she essentially let go, dying two days after she entered hospice care.

Duane visited her the night before she died, and gave her a kiss on the forehead, but he wasn't sure she was aware of his presence, or his kiss.

The funeral was the next day. Jenny was not religious. A lot of people liked her, though, and the burial was well attended.

"Us old-timers are thinning out quick now," Bobby Lee said. "At least she lived long enough to see my record bass."

Then he began to cry.

Duane was feeling a little shaky inside himself.

There were fewer and fewer people in Thalia now that he even knew.

"We fucked a good bit, up in that croppie shack up at Lake Kemp," Bobby Lee said. "That's human nature, ain't it?"

"That's human nature," Duane agreed.

ANNIE QUIT US," Dickie mentioned—his wife was out of town and he
and Duane were grilling steaks. Duane was drinking a little Bourbon
but Dickie restricted himself to Evian water. His years of addiction were
not forgotten.

"If I caused it, I'm sorry," Duane said.

"Forget it, I've already found someone just as good or better," Dickie
said. "Her name is Dal—she's from Thailand, most recently."

"Annie was smart but Dal is super-smart," Dickie said. "We won't lose
a step."

"Good—I'll try not to marry Dal."

"If I wasn't married *I'd* try to marry her," Dickie said. "She's in the
Emirates just now but she'll be along soon."

That night, restless, Duane climbed up on the observation deck—still
the *only* observation deck—and had a drink with Boyd and Bobby.

"I'm having a harder and harder time feeling smart, in this modern
world," he said. "How about you Boyd—do you still feel smart?"

"Mostly," Boyd said.

"Maybe you aren't smart anymore, Duane," Bobby suggested. "You
used to kinda run this whole part of the country, and now you don't."

"That was forty years back," Duane said. "And what I ran turned out
not to amount to much."

"I'd rather be useful than smart," Boyd said. "And right now I don't feel
very damn useful. I did catch a glimpse of that porn star who works for
Dickie, though."

"You're luckier than me, Boyd," Bobby Lee said. "My glimpse cost me
over a hundred dollars in traffic fines."

When Duane left he was halfway down the ladder when he realized he was
much too drunk to be climbing down high ladders in the night. By being very
careful he made it the rest of the way down. Once down he headed for town.

"Hey," Bobby Lee yelled, when he saw Duane heading back to Thalia. "You're going the wrong way. Your cabin's in the other direction."

"I'm not going to my cabin—I need to go to the Kwik-Sack and buy an atlas," Duane yelled.

He had developed a sudden desire to know where Thailand was—the place the mysterious Dal was coming from. He was almost to the city limits before he realized that the only atlas the Kwik-Sack might have would just show the U.S., Mexico and Canada.

It had been a while since Duane had been drunk enough to make that kind of mistake.

He went to his big house and lay in the hot tub a long time before he felt sober enough even to go to bed.

49

To HIS ANNOYANCE Duane entered a phase in which his eyes would fill up and spill over. The first time it happened—he was buying peanut butter at the Kwik-Sack—he put it down to ragweed allergy. But after it had happened two or three times, he realized that he was crying. Not sobbing deeply, or crying for long; nothing like that. But, undeniably, he was subject to little spurts of crying.

When, embarrassed, he told Ethel at the Kwik-Sack that he must be allergic to ragweed, Ethel corrected him.

"It's the oak pollen that's getting you, honey," she said. "The ragweed's over for the year."

Ethel chain-smoked, in bold defiance of a new city ordinance prohibiting smoking inside buildings.

Duane was careful to hide his little spoutings of tears from everyone, and, since he kept largely to himself, he succeeded. The few who saw him looking red-eyed put it down to ragweed, or oak pollen or Johnson grass.

Often, when he walked home out to his cabin, Double Aught would pick him up a little way north of the tower and accompany him home. On these strolls Double Aught always stayed on the west side of the fence, which was why it had been such a shock, the day Casey Kincaid had casually shooed him away, that Double Aught had been on the *east* of the fence. And he had got there, apparently, without trampling down the fence around the pasture to the west. How?

"Wire cutters, that's how," Boyd Cotton said, when Duane asked him what he thought of this occurrence. "You wouldn't notice unless you really ride the line, like K.K. wants me to do, but meth dealers have probably cut the wire in fifteen or twenty places around the perimeter of the big pasture, and they don't bother to repair the cuts, particularly not this time of year, with the weeds so high. Rhinos find the cuts. But most of them seem content to stay in the big pasture, and why not? It's where the hay racks are."

Boyd looked wistful for a moment—a way Duane had never seen him look.

"When I was sixteen I rode line for the Matador Ranch—back when the Matador was the biggest ranch in that part of Texas."

"Everybody's heard of the Matador—even oilfielders like me," Duane said.

"Now I'm old and I'm riding line again, for a ranch with thirty-nine rhinos so far. The Matador ran more than one hundred thousand cattle. But it got split up and those days are gone."

"Long gone," Duane said.

"Now here I am old and here I am riding line again," Boyd said. "It makes me think I didn't advance very far. I had the skills to do more but the opportunity passed."

Bobby Lee had sat silent during this dialogue—then, suddenly, to their amazement, he burst into tears.

"You two are lucky," he said, when the tear burst passed. "You both once had skills, but I never had anything except the skill to shack up with women who shoot holes in me later on. Now here I am old, and I was never fit for much of anything."

"Bobby Lee, hush," Boyd said, sharply. "Feeling sorry for yourself is a bad habit. Just hush!"

"Okay," Bobby Lee said—and he did hush.

"Come ride the line with me tomorrow," Boyd said to Duane. "Maybe we can find where your pet rhino got out."

"Him?" Bobby Lee said. "He's an oilman. He's never been on a horse in his life."

"First time for everything," Boyd said.

Nobody disagreed.

BOYD COTTON FAVORED an early start. So did Duane. He walked from the cabin to the tower in off-the-shelf boots he had purchased the day before. They could use a little breaking in.

As he neared the tower he heard an airplane, and looked up to see the familiar white Cessna belonging to K.K. Slater. The boss lady was arriving. He was glad he had taken the trouble to shave, though Boyd Cotton had not; Boyd had batched most of his life, and had not made shaving much of a priority.

When he walked into the headquarters area K.K. Slater was already mounted on her bay thoroughbred. Boyd had saddled his top quarter horse and another, bulkier animal for Duane.

"You get the plug, Duane," K.K. said. She and Boyd watched critically as Duane, no cowboy, managed an awkward mount. Still, he was on the horse, and as ready as he would ever be to ride a line.

Boyd and K.K. sat for a moment, perhaps considering the question of precedence. Who should lead, the boss lady or the top hand?

"You lead, Boyd," K.K. said. "You know this pasture and I don't."

"It's big enough we could probably manage side by side without even spooking your thoroughbred," Boyd said.

"Let's do it," K.K. said. "And Duane on his plug can eat our dust."

51

BOYD TOOK THEM west about twenty yards inside the fence line, close enough that even Duane could see what tracks were near the fence. Boyd traveled at an easy trot, rapid enough to cover the ground but slow enough to see anything that might require them to stop, examine and consult.

Once in a while K.K. would look back at Duane and smile.

"You okay?" she asked.

"Oh sure—I always meant to ride a horse sometime in my life, and now I have."

Now and then, as they rode, they saw a rhino or two in the distance. Once they saw four together. The rhinos seemed at ease in the grassy plains country. One rhino, a yearling, scampered over toward the horsemen, but then turned tail and hurried back to his mother.

"The little boy smelled us," K.K. said. "They don't have very good vision. That was Leo, our baby."

When they got about halfway around the big pasture they came to a little man-made pond—what was called a lake by most locals. The water was brown and shallow, and the heads of perhaps a dozen turtles poked up out of the water. The shallows were thick with rhino tracks.

"Several of them water here but not Duane's pet," Boyd said. He loosened his reins so his horse could drink. The thoroughbred shied a time or two before he stepped into the water.

Duane's plug waded way in and drank noisily.

"I'd go skinny-dipping," K.K. said. "But somehow you gents don't seem like the skinny-dipping type."

By the time they had ridden a wide circle and were headed back toward the tower they had inspected most of the rhino herd—thirty-seven out of thirty-nine, by Boyd's count.

One rhino they didn't see was Double Aught, the one who had the least fear of humans.

"You think he's out?" K.K. asked.

"Yep," Boyd said.

"Then where's he getting out?"

"Good question," Boyd said. "There's no sign that he's been near the fence."

"Very curious," K.K. said. "Could we have missed the sign?"

Boyd looked at her solemnly and K.K. smiled and didn't repeat the question.

K.K. looked at Duane.

"When he follows you home which pasture does he walk in?" she asked.

Duane thought for a few minutes and realized he had no proper answer. Usually he was beyond the west fence, but not always. The most singular thing about his appearance was that he would suddenly just be *there*.

"I ought to know, but I don't," Duane said. "Seems like he disappears."

"Maybe somebody's letting him out one of the gates," she suggested.

"Nope, I looked—he ain't been through any of our gates," Boyd said, "But the fence gets cut in a lot of places now."

"Well, how odd," K.K. said, as they rode home.

52

WHEN THEY GOT back to the tower Boyd unsaddled his quarter horse and turned him loose so he could have a roll in the dirt.

K.K. looked at Boyd coolly.

"That's not my way," she said—then she proceeded to rub down her thoroughbred. When she finished she looked at Boyd and Duane.

"Something wrong on the Rhino Ranch," she said. "I don't know what it is, and neither do you."

"Do you suppose a critter as big as Double Aught could jump the fence?" Duane asked.

"Probably, but not without leaving tracks," Boyd said.

"When did you see the big boy last?" K.K. asked Duane.

"Last night," Duane said.

"He might have jumped out," Boyd said. "I've seen bulls jump a lot higher than you'd think a bull could jump."

"Big animals can do pretty much anything they want to," K.K. said. "I mean, they can if they're excited enough."

"Why would Double Aught be excited enough to jump a fence?" Duane wondered.

"I've seen my share of bulls jump quite a few things—ditches and creeks and fences—but every single one of them had left a track."

"Rhinos don't fly—that's what I know," K.K. said.

Just at that moment her cell phone rang. She picked it up impatiently and listened for a minute.

"No, that can't be," she said loudly. "That simply *cannot* be," she went on. "The rhino was here yesterday. This is simply some mistake." She clicked off the cell phone and stuck it in her pocket. Then she glared at Boyd and Duane, as if whatever had happened was their fault.

"A rhinoceros was sighted near Amarillo," she told them. "He was standing by I-40, watching the trucks go by."

"Have they caught him?" Boyd asked.

"That's the odd part," K.K. said. "They didn't catch him. He's disap-peared. Several hundred people claim to have seen him but no one has any idea where he is now."

"That's plains country—you think he'd be easy to spot," Boyd said.

"You'd think," K.K said. "Could I sleep in your guest room tonight, Duane? I need to stay around until I sort this out."

"Sure," Duane said. "You're welcome even if you ain't quiet as a mouse." K.K. sighed.

"If there's one thing I learned in Africa it's that great animals can do things you would never expect them to do," she said.

No one spoke for a while, but all three of them thought about great animals, and what they might do.

"I suspect that's true," Boyd said. "Though it's not been my good for-tune to work with many great animals—mainly I've just worked with shitty-assed cows.

"I'd like to see Africa sometime," he added. Duane had never heard Boyd Cotton express a desire to travel before.

"I know Double Aught is a great animal," Duane said. "But, even so, could he really make it from here to Amarillo in one night?"

"I don't really know, but the fact is I'm getting my chicken-fried steak urge," she said. "Any takers? It's my night to pay."

They all went and they all ate, but Duane could not get Double Aught off his mind. There was a dearth of conversation, which probably meant that the other two couldn't, either.

WHEN THEY GOT to Duane's house K.K. took a shower, emerging finally wearing an old bathrobe she had found, by which time the question of Double Aught's appearance in Amarillo had been explained by several news channels. The big rhinoceros standing by I-40 proved to be an inflatable replica of Double Aught, which two rodeo promoters had had made by the company that made inflatable King Kongs to hang over the opening of car lots and such.

The promoters owned up and Double Aught was deflated and hauled off in a horse trailer. For years to come, however, the inflatable rhino would often be used as a float at Panhandle rodeos, until a bucking bull with his dander up took a run at it and ripped it to shreds.

Of more immediate interest to the news channels was a terrible electrical storm, the worst ever seen in the Panhandle, which did extensive damage. Sixty-three cows at a dairy near Dalhart were struck dead by one lightning bolt: big news in the Dalhart area.

"It still doesn't explain where Double Aught is now," K.K. pointed out, before she went to bed.

54

BOTH BOBBY LEE and Boyd were drinking more, mainly because dealing with all the journalists who came to stake out Double Aught's home caused their nerves to fray. "I've been asked more questions today than I've been asked in the last sixty years put together," Bobby Lee said.

"Right," Boyd said. "How would we know where a runaway rhino would go?"

"I think I see Duane coming, on foot," Boyd said. "I expect he misses his walks and his walking buddy too."

When he drew even with the tower Duane gave the two of them a wave, but didn't stop to visit. He wanted to get on to his cabin, in case his grandson, the soon-to-be Rhodes Scholar, showed up.

A mile farther and Duane began to feel strange. It was a dark night—dark enough to be a little nervous about snakes—but he kept walking.

No snakes appeared but there was something large ahead of him, and not far ahead.

Then Double Aught grunted a time or two—not loud, but firmly.

"Welcome back yourself," Duane said.

DOUBLE AUGHT stood there placidly, barely ten yards from Duane. Duane felt a deep relief, deeper than he would have been able to explain.

But he also felt concern. Double Aught was now unquestionably the most famous rhino in the world. Dozens of people with mentalities no different from that of the Colorado roughnecks were driving the country roads of Texas, New Mexico and Oklahoma. Rhino patrols had even been organized in some small towns in the region, and most of their members were of a mind-set to shoot on sight, whether Double Aught had done anything threatening or not.

It occurred to Duane that Double Aught might be hungry—and if he could be lured back to the hay rack he would have Bobby Lee and Boyd to keep an eye on him.

"The safest place for you, my friend, is the Rhino Ranch," and he immediately started walking back along the road he had just come up. As if to prove Duane's hunger theory, Double Aught's stomach rumbled a time or two.

On the walk back to the observation tower Duane began to ponder an element of the situation that had not occurred to him before. In taking Double Aught home, as it were, he was ignoring the fact that the rhino's real home was in Kenya. Maybe his big friend was homesick. Alfalfa hay might be tasty enough but food and home were different. If it turned out that Double Aught had actually gone anywhere, maybe he had been looking for Kenya.

It was a thought that put a new twist on the matter.

56

"**S**ON OF A BITCH," Boyd Cotton said. "Look who's coming up the road."

"If it's who I think it is I don't really want to know," Bobby Lee said, but a second later he reversed himself and looked. There was Duane and Double Aught, coming through the gate of the compound, which Duane had opened.

In a moment Double Aught was munching contentedly on some fresh alfalfa hay.

"Where'd you find him, Duane?" Boyd asked.

"I guess we found each other," Duane said. "Up near my cabin."

"When I hired on for this job I figured I'd be a kind of cowboy," Bobby Lee said. "I was thinking rhinos must be pretty much like cattle. They both have four legs and all.

"But I guess they aren't like cattle at all," he said. "So where does that leave us, Boyd?"

"Confused, but that's not fatal," Boyd said.

L ATER DUANE TALKED to Willy about the return of Double Aught.

"I guess you two have got something going," Willy said. "As far as I know there's no reason why a human couldn't be friends with a rhino."

"It's not exactly that we're friends," Duane said. "It's more like he's my brother."

"Wow," Willy said. "The brother you never had?"

"I did have a brother—I nearly forget it sometimes, since he died at birth."

"I don't think anyone ever told me that," Willy said.

"I'm not sure your mother even knows about it—or your aunt, either."

"Wow," Willy said, again. "I'm going to have to think about this."

58

D UANE WAS IN the big house, trying to balance his checkbook, when Casey Kinkaid walked in the door. She wore a shirt with little ties in front, exposing her navel and her young belly.

"I hope you're watching your calendar, Mr. Moore," she said. "I finally turned eighteen. Mind if I use your bathroom?"

"Go right ahead," Duane said, courteously, though he found Casey's sudden arrival more than a little alarming. A few minutes later, when she walked into his kitchen stark naked, his alarm intensified.

"Tah dah!" she said, spreading her arms and legs.

Without moving, or so much as touching her, Duane could easily believe that Casey would make a successful porn star. She had, for starters, what most viewers would believe to be a perfect body—a 10 on a scale of 10, like in the movie of that name.

"I'm not fucking that airman with the big dick anymore," Casey mentioned. She looked down at him, where he sat with a bank statement and a pile of checks.

"I mean, you don't need to be intimidated by the size of Joe's dick," she said. "It works better for making porn than it does in real life."

She walked around the table and spread her legs even wider. What was there to be seen, he could easily see.

"The one thing I don't like about making porn is having to shave your pussy," Casey said. "Producers say pubic hair hides too much, but what do they know?

"While I've been waiting to turn eighteen you've kind of grown on me, Mr. Moore," Casey said. "That's why I'm standing here naked, feeling my pussy getting wet. I'm real well lubricated usually, when I fuck," she added.

Then she dropped to her knees, unbuckled Duane's jeans and gave him a blow job, a treat he had not had in a while. He kept thinking he ought to stop it—the girl was barely Willy's age—but before he could take evasive action he came and the blow job was over.

"How's that, little buddy?" she said, addressing his prick. "If I were a guy I'd never wear underwear—too hard to get a stiff dick out of underwear, and then the underwear gets all yucky unless the girl is real good at swallowing all the cum."

Then she giggled.

"Gee, I kind of raped you, didn't I, Mr. Moore?"

Then she came out from under the table and headed for the bathroom again. Just as she emerged, dressed, the phone rang, but Duane didn't answer it. He just sat, amid his checks.

"Probably your other girlfriend, that's why you're not answering that phone," Casey said. She bent, kissed him lightly on the lips and left.

Duane knew he had just permitted something to happen that was clearly very foolish. Maybe Casey really was eighteen—but it could also be that she was just sixteen. His role had been passive but that wouldn't matter much if Casey decided to blackmail him. It would be the talk of the region. The one bright spot was that she couldn't have gotten pregnant—not from what they had just done.

The other side of the coin was that he hadn't had sex in a while, and getting that unexpected blow job had felt very good.

He was an aging man—how many chances was he likely to get for casual pleasure of that sort? A blow job might never come his way again.

Besides that, the truth was he *liked* Casey. He had enjoyed what happened, and he would enjoy it if it should happen again.

Whether he would actively try to *make* it happen again—with all the risks it involved—was something he would have to think about.

For the moment, balancing his checkbook just didn't match his mood, so he put rubber bands around the piles of checks and left that tedious task for another day.

THE CALL DUANE had ignored was from Dickie. Instead of returning it Duane got in his pickup and rode the twenty miles to the company offices in Wichita Falls.

When he walked into the office the first thing he saw was a small-boned, neat Asian woman who sat in front of the main bank of computers. Her black hair was cut very short, and there was a delicacy about her movements that impressed Duane very much. She did not look at him.

This woman, Duane knew, must be Dal.

"Yep, that's her," Dickie said. "I don't like to interrupt her when she's concentrating—I'll introduce her later."

"She was a boat person," he added. "She's seen rough times."

"How old is she?" Duane asked. "I wouldn't have thought she was old enough to be a boat person."

"She was," Dickie said.

"What brings you over here in the heat of the day?" Dickie asked.

"I did something bad," Duane said.

Dickie laughed, a nice deep laugh.

"No you didn't, Daddy," he said. "You just had sex with Casey," he said. "So have plenty of others."

"But not you?"

"Not me because my dear wife, Annette, would chop me into little pieces if the news got back to her, which it would."

"I don't see Casey anywhere—did she quit?" Duane asked.

"Fired," Dickie said. "It was inevitable, given her habits. I caught her having phone sex with the president of a very large bank—a man crucial to our financing, and the father, I believe, of six children."

"Did she leave town?"

"Not yet," Dickie said. "She's probably over there right now having phone sex with some of her other customers."

"Can she make money doing phone sex?" Duane asked.

"About a thousand a day, net, she claims," Dickie said. "She's said to be very good at making sucking sounds."

"This is not the world I was born into," Duane said. "But it may be that my little lapse didn't do any real damage."

"No damage, probably," Dickie said. "Nearly everybody could use some kind of sex now and then. Even me, but then I've got Annette and her sharp grubbing hoe to think of."

When they came out of the office Dal was staring just as intently at the bank of computers.

"She's in a zone," Dickie said. "We might just want to save the introductions for next time."

"Does she have children?"

"Four—two dead, two alive," Dickie said.

Though he lingered a few minutes, Duane did not meet Dal. The time was just not right.

THINGS TOOK A serious downturn at the Rhino Ranch when three rhinos died within a week: an old female, past breeding age, a young female and a middle-aged male. These deaths represented an immense setback for the program. Double Aught vanished from the papers, to be replaced by learned opinion from the best rhino vets in America— brought in by K.K. Slater, who called Duane and asked if she could stay in his house again; the vets and publicity people would find lodgings in Wichita Falls.

"Maybe I'll grill you a real steak for a change," he suggested.

"That would be nice," K.K. said. "Has Boyd Cotton ever had a girl-friend?"

The question surprised him.

"Well, I believe he married twice but both wives died. I'm not sure he's ever had what you would call a girlfriend."

"Didn't think so," K.K. said. "This is bad about the rhinos, though not unexpected."

"Why would it be expected?"

"Because they're complicated, with tricky digestive systems, which makes them hard to translocate. Relocation efforts had been made before, but never with much success. They dehydrate easily."

"What will you do?"

"Make some mud wallows, for starters," she said.

"So far we've lost four out of forty," she said.

"It still leaves you thirty-six."

"Not enough," K.K. said, and hung up.

61

THE CESSNA ARRIVED at dusk. Duane had expected to see Myles and various of the vets, but K.K. came alone, and said little as Duane drove her the short distance to his house.

While K.K. cleaned up he grilled two thick steaks, procured from a local butcher he trusted, baked two potatoes, sliced some tomatoes from his own garden.

K.K. had arrived none too clean—she'd been working with a young filly all day and didn't take time to change until she arrived at Duane's.

"Sometimes the thought of making even the slightest effort to be lady-like pisses me off," she said. "Do you know who the San are?"

"'Fraid not," Duane admitted.

"They're usually called Bushmen," she said, "though some consider that racist now. They are a tribe of small people who live, most of them, in the Kalahari Game Preserve, which is a precarious place to live if you're hunter-gatherers, like the San."

"Okay," Duane said.

"I'm thinking of bringing one here," K.K. said. "If I do I would appreciate it if you kind of keep an eye on him, for a while."

"Does he speak English?"

"Heavens no," she said. "The San speak a click language, very hard to learn. The ones I've met are very shy, and they're maybe the best trackers in the world.

"There's one I call Sam," she went on. "He calls me Jack. The San are more sensitive to animals than any native people I've ever met. They've learned to use a global tracking device. Mainly they know when something's wrong with an animal. If Sam had been here maybe the three rhinos wouldn't have died."

"Well, bring him—I'll try to help."

"I guess we just got off to a bad start somehow, Duane," she said. "Why did we?"

"I'm prickly around rich people," he said.

He got up and brought coffee. K.K. had eaten every bit of her meal. When he set her coffee in front of her she poured a little more bourbon into it.

"Could Double Aught still breed?" Duane asked.

"With him it doesn't matter," she said. "We must have at least a gallon of his sperm stored up.

"And since we're on the subject, consider this fact: I myself have been celibate for seven years."

Duane could not repress a moment of anxiety but K.K. patted his hand.

"Don't panic, honey . . . it's Boyd Cotton I want," she said.

Duane had not been as taken by K.K.'s celibacy announcement as she might have thought. In a dim way he had more or less known it. He had been in the company of Boyd and K.K. to have sensed the interest, and there was nothing to be surprised about. Boyd Cotton was a compelling man. Karla Moore, Duane's dead wife, had several times mentioned what an attractive man Boyd Cotton was.

"Boyd's standoffish, but I suppose your chances would be as good as the next woman's," he said.

"In other words, slim to none," K.K. said.

"I wouldn't say none, but I agree about slim," he said.

SAM OF THE SAN traveled light. He wore a loincloth, carried a sack of sorts over his shoulder, had a tiny bow and quiver with five or six arrows in it and was barefoot. The only thing that seemed to place him in the modern age was his global positioning device, which he kept in a little holster, clipped to his loincloth.

He arrived by helicopter and the whole Rhino Enterprises crew was there to greet him: K.K., Myles, Bobby Lee, Boyd, the Hartman brothers and Duane—an honorary guest. Though not really part of Rhino Enterprises, he did not want to miss the arrival of the first Bushman to ever appear in Thalia County.

To Duane, Sam seemed even smaller than Dal, but he moved with the same delicacy. He smiled as he got out of the helicopter but then went right to work. He marched over to Double Aught, who was standing with a female near the hay racks, which were stuffed with fresh alfalfa.

The small man spoke in his click language a minute or two, and what he said seemed to startle—perhaps even admonish—the rhinos, both of whom huffed before they trotted away.

"Now I've seen a miracle," Bobby Lee said. "A man who can talk to rhinos and be understood."

"Sam disapproves of much of what we do," K.K. admitted. "He thinks the rhinos should forage for their food, like they do in Africa.

"Life is not easy for the San," she went on. "They live in a hard place—not unreasonably, they consider us wasteful slobs."

"Who's he gonna shoot with that bow and arrow?" Dub Hartman asked.

"The arrows are poisoned, of course," K.K. mentioned. "One of those arrows will kill the largest antelope—not immediately, but eventually. But the San are a patient people. They can wait for the antelope to drop."

As they watched, Sam of the San walked away, in the direction the two rhinos had gone.

"Well, Sam's here, that's a relief," K.K. said. "How about taking me to lunch, Boyd? I hear there's a place in Seymour that's good."

"Hop into my chariot," Boyd said, meaning his pickup.

It was as if he had been expecting the question. A minute later they were gone.

"Life's getting stranger," Bobby Lee said. "When do you reckon that little man will come back?"

"Now how would I know?" Duane said.

There was a shed near the tower that contained a couple of off-road vehicles and a variety of tools.

"Myles says he's gonna live in that shed," Bobby said. "He said that in Africa his whole family just lives by a bush.

"I guess the boss lady is going to seduce old Boyd," he added.

"Doubtful," Duane said, before walking off toward his cabin. He had enjoyed seeing Sam of the San, but he had no interest in speculating about K.K. and Boyd.

For one thing, he had a romantic quandary of his own to consider. Casey Kincaid had struck, and he was not finding it easy to forget her easy sexuality. He liked Casey and had begun to look forward to seeing her again, though he still had the uneasy feeling that a rather big bill might be presented someday. At present he was yo-yoing between apprehension and desire.

It was the kind of situation that called for wise counsel, and the wisest counsel he had available to him was Honor Carmichael, who was in Maine when he called.

"I feel guilty when I call you about things like this," he said.

"Oh, don't," she said. "If I didn't want to talk to you I'd just change my number."

"Okay," Duane said. "Casey Kincaid gave me a blow job."

"If that's all she did, forget it, and if she gives you another one, enjoy it," Honor advised.

"Well, I sure enjoyed the first one, but I've got a bad feeling that something's coming along that I'm not going to enjoy all that much."

"Like pregnancy, you mean?" Honor asked.

"Yep."

"I think I'm going back to my retirement, Duane," Honor said. "You'll just have to handle this yourself."

And she hung up.

Duane felt disappointed. Usually when he talked to Honor he felt better for their just having talked. This time he just felt anxious.

64

"**A** BUSHMAN IN THALIA?" Willy said, when his grandfather called to report. "That's cool. I guess I'll miss him, though. I'll be off to England tomorrow."

Duane felt a sag inside. Willy had always been a major ally.

"Let me know when you get settled," he said. "It's kind of weird around here now, between the Bushman and the porn star. Plus Dickie has hired an Asian woman to replace Annie. I haven't met her yet."

There was a pause.

"Are you involved with that porn star?" Willy asked.

"I don't think so, but there are some gray areas," he admitted. "I might have made a little mistake, but I didn't get anybody pregnant."

"I hope you keep it that way," Willy said. "If you got somebody pregnant it would totally freak my mom out—and my aunt too."

"There's nothing to worry about on that score," Duane said. "Enjoy England."

65

AFTER THE DEATHS of the three rhinos and the strange escape of Double Aught—if such an escape actually happened—Boyd Cotton had started riding the line a lot, sometimes in daylight, sometimes at night.

This left Bobby Lee alone on the tower, and he had never been particularly happy alone.

"It wouldn't hurt you to stop and visit with me a little while, if you're on the way to your cabin," he told Duane.

"I've been visiting with you for nearly sixty years—why *wouldn't* I stop and visit?"

"Yeah but you haven't been seeing Casey for sixty years," Bobby said. "You might be pussy-whipped, and if you're pussy-whipped you might not feel up to climbing the damn ladder.

"You might be too pussy-whipped to help out an old friend who's lonely."

It was a curious admission on Bobby Lee's part.

Indeed, Duane himself had begun to feel lonely from time to time. Much of his life had been lived in the midst of a mob: first his family, and then his derrick crews.

Duane was so unfamiliar with loneliness that, once he began to suffer from it, it took him several months to identify it. The fact was, he had come to like the company of people—even people he once would have been unable to tolerate.

He knew that his lifelong friend Bobby Lee must be lonely from time to time. He had no steady woman, now that Jenny Marlow was dead. But the fact was, Bobby Lee had seemed lonely nearly all his life.

"I know we've visited a lot, Duane," Bobby said. "But now we're old and life's different."

"Well, we're not *real* old yet," Duane pointed out; he wanted to counter the notion that he was exactly old.

"There is one big problem with old," Bobby said.

"What would that be?"

"It ain't reversible," Bobby Lee said. "I don't think we're the first two friends in the world who might end up getting younger."

"You've got a point," Duane said. "And that concludes our visit for tonight. I believe I'll keep on walking."

66

The next afternoon, while he was sitting under his tree, reading a few pages of *Desert Solitaire*, K.K. Slater drove up in Boyd Cotton's pickup.

She parked outside the gate and walked over to where Duane sat.

"Driving Boyd's old pickup takes me back to my girlhood," K.K. said. "Hell, it was practically made in my girlhood. Are you still reading Ed Abbey?"

"I'm not exactly reading—I'm more just sitting here with a book."

"I was never a reader," K.K. admitted. "I thought I'd come by and see that you were staying out of trouble."

"I guess I'm about as out of trouble as I can get," he said. "I was sort of hoping Double Aught would pay me a visit, but so far he hasn't."

"That's probably because Sam annoyed him yesterday," she said. "When he's annoyed he hides out. Even though he weighs nearly five thousand pounds he can make himself hard to spot.

"Sam has the odd notion that animals should do what he wants them to do," she said.

"Where is Sam?"

"No idea," she said. "Sam goes where he pleases, and that's an understatement.

"Boyd Cotton wants to take helicopter lessons," she said.

"Helicopter lessons?" Duane said, astonished.

"Sure. In the first place helicopters are handy for locating animals—and in the second place I think Boyd is scared a rhino might get one of his horses."

"I expect they might," Duane said, still surprised. Boyd Cotton flying a helicopter? That was certainly a change.

"**T**HE HARTMAN TWINS quit us," Bobby Lee told Duane, on their next visit—it was about sundown.

"Why?"

"They're scared of that little man with the poison arrows," Bobby said. "They didn't like being out here, anyway—too far from Thalia."

"Too far from Thalia?" Duane asked. "Thalia's right there, in plain sight."

"It's outside the city limits, though," Bobby pointed out. "There's some people who don't feel safe outside the city limits of Thalia."

"I guess so," Duane said. "Most normal people think it's dull as hell, but it sure hits the spot with Dub and Bub."

68

THE NEXT MORNING Duane got up early and drove to the Asia Wonder Deli, where to his astonishment he found Sam of the San, talking with Mike and Tommy in sign. His small hands were a blur of motion.

Duane got a couple of spring rolls and settled down to eat them.

"Tommy lived in Botswana," Mike told Duane. "He knows many San." Then Mike frowned.

"Well, there are not many San now, but Tommy did know some."

"I'm too slow for sign talk," Mike admitted. "When they get through, Tommy will translate."

From time to time a few roughnecks would wander in to get some Asian breakfast; they were startled to see Sam of the San, and, like the Hartman twins, took note of the bow and arrows. Sam had also acquired some kind of digging stick, which he left in his lap as his hands told their stories.

Over his shoulder he carried several roots.

"To eat," Mike said, when Duane asked about the roots. "The San are very good at sniffing out edible roots."

"But he's never been here before—how does he know what's edible and what isn't?"

"They are fine smellers," Mike said, and left it at that.

"Big chance to take," one young roughneck said.

"You are not San," Mike reminded him. "Their whole life is a big chance."

Duane saw that Sam was eating spring rolls.

"Does Sam pay you?" he asked.

"Of course," Mike said. "This morning he brought us a nice wild piglet."

"I think there is bad news from the Rhino Ranch, though," Mike said. "That big rhino that likes you, he's gone."

"Uh-oh," Duane said.

"I don't know for sure," Mike said. The San talk too fast—I don't get it all."

"I guess we better hurry back to the ranch and see what they think," he said.

"We cook that little piglet—be ready Sunday," Mike said. "Very tasty."

"I'll be here," Duane said.

69

NEWS THAT DOUBLE AUGHT was gone again tilted Duane in a direction he didn't really want to go. Instead of going back to the Rhino Ranch, he turned right instead of left and in less than fifteen minutes found himself at Casey Kincaid's door. She lived in a rather sedate apartment complex, in one of the best neighborhoods in Wichita Falls. Just as he raised his hand to knock, she opened the door.

"Took you long enough, you old fart," she said. She was dressed in a T-shirt and a thong.

"It's because I have so many scruples to overcome," he told her. It was true, but Casey could take it as a joke, if she wanted to.

So far she had not invited him in.

"You're older than I remember you being," she said. "I don't know about this. Some old guys croak when they're fucking. You croaking would be about the last thing I need."

But then she made a gesture with her head, which he took to mean he was invited in.

"I only do phone sex for money, Mr. Moore," she said. "Real sex I only do if there's something interesting about the guy.

"All I see that's interesting about you is your guilt," she told him.

It was not the response Duane had been expecting, but it was an interesting response, anyway. Even as she spoke he was experiencing some guilt. What was he doing in the apartment of this young woman, who, for a goodly number of reasons, was an inappropriate sexual partner for him to become involved with?

Casey watched him with a blank expression on her face.

Then, as if she were conducting an experiment of her own conception, she slowly took off her T-shirt.

"Oh, well, Mr. Moore," she said. "You're here and nobody else in the

way of a male is. Let's get naked and see if we can think of anything interesting to do."

Guilty or not, it was what Duane wanted her to say. He began to take
off his clothes.

GUYS ARE SORT of amazing to me, when I start to think about how stupid they are," Casey said. They had done various things, and were resting.

"Probably it's smarter not to think about men at all," she said.

"Why not?" he asked.

"Who wants to waste their youth and beauty on totally brainless guys," she said. "Like the two fat-dick brothers who worked for the rhino place. They showed up one night and offered me money, as if I were a cheap whore. I told them I was an actress, not a whore—if they go home and call me we could do phone sex—at least we could if they could put it on their credit card."

"And what did they do?"

"Went home and called me and I did my cocksucking sound a few times and they shot right off.

"I never let any of you yokels touch my asshole," Casey said. "It's too sensitive to trust to amateurs. I only butt-fuck with my peers."

"Do you have many?"

"Sure, but not around here. Do you ever wonder why I haven't really let you penetrate me yet?"

"I noticed it hadn't happened," Duane said.

"And it won't happen, unless you get a vasectomy first."

Duane was stunned. A vasectomy first?

"I guess I've never given much thought to vasectomies," he said.

"I've had several guys do it," she said. "I'm the snip doctor's best shill, Mr. Moore."

Duane pondered that news for a bit. He felt some inner resistance to having a vasectomy.

"It's just a little snip," she said. "Surely the chance to fuck me is worth a little snip."

Duane didn't bite.

"If you just did it we could enjoy a lot of things we haven't enjoyed yet," she said. "I'm talking about all those things nobody bothered to teach you."

When he got home he sat under his tree with his book, but didn't read it. He was pretty sure there was nothing in it about vasectomies.

DUANE SHOWED UP at the office one morning when Dal's computer was down—it gave him his first real chance to introduce himself to her, which he did.

Dal greeted him with a shy smile.

"I'm glad you're working for us," Duane said.

"I am glad also," Dal said.

"They still haven't found Double Aught," Dickie said, taking his cell phone from his ear for a moment.

"I don't know why he keeps running off," Duane said.

"Let him go, sir—they are bad animals," Dal said.

Duane was startled. Bad animals. Why?

"The one that's lost had kind of made friends with me," he told her, but Dal shook her head.

"You may think so, sir, but it is not true," she insisted.

Duane felt off balance—Dal was vehement, which he had not expected. He had been prepared to like Dal, and he did like her, but he wondered why she was so emphatic about rhinos. He knew they had them in Asia too, though not many.

"Any special reason for thinking so?" he asked.

Dal saw a flicker from her computer and looked at it briefly before turning back to Duane.

"I think you will have to go very far to find this beast who is not your friend," she said, and turned back to her screen.

72

"I THINK THEY'VE FOUND a way to drill in the Barnett Shale," Dickie told his father one morning. "It's going to change everything."

Duane shrugged.

"I've heard about the Barnett Shale all my life," he said. "I've been told many, many times about techniques that were going to change everything. Of course there are booms and busts. But so far nothing that's come along has really changed everything."

"You have to drill horizontally, which they couldn't in your time but can easily do now."

"Dal's been sifting through some old findings and she thinks the Barnett Shale might show up in two or three of them. It might be as close as Montague County, where we've never drilled."

"We did drill there a couple of times in the Fifties," Duane told him. "We just hit the Caddo sand, as usual."

Then he noticed that Dickie wasn't really listening. He was looking out the window—Casey Kincaid was walking across the parking lot. Wherever she went she seemed to draw all eyes.

Dal, though, was not watching Casey at all. She was staring intently at her computer, and Duane had no intention of interrupting her.

Still, sometime when she wasn't so busy he wanted to ask her again, about the matter of Double Aught.

73

THE NORTH TOWER at the Rhino Ranch had become a place of low moods.

Duane heard that K.K. was flying up. As he was walking by he saw Boyd Cotton about to mount his quarter horse and go ride the line.

"Sam may know something," Boyd said, as he mounted. "But if he does he's keeping it to himself," Boyd added. "It's worrying me that Double Aught don't leave a track. I've been following four-legged animals all my life and every single one of them has left a track.

"I like my jobs to make sense, and this one don't," Boyd said.

After which he left.

"Boyd thinks Double Aught might be a ghost," Bobby Lee said, the minute Boyd rode off.

"I wonder what Sam thinks?"

"Whatever it is we won't know it until Tommy comes over for a chat," Bobby Lee said.

Then the familiar white Cessna circled and landed.

"Working here was exciting at first, but now it ain't," Bobby said. "How's life with Casey?"

"She wants me to get a vasectomy," Duane said.

"If you do it you'll never be the same," Bobby said.

"But I'll never be the same, anyway," Duane said. "Old people get less and less the same, all the time."

"Don't I know it, it's them dying brain cells," Bobby Lee said.

74

"THERE'S BEEN a sighting," Honor Carmichael announced.

Duane, who had been napping, was confused.

"Of Double Aught?" he asked. "Where is he?"

"Not of the stupid rhinoceros—I mean of your most recent wife and her new best friend."

Duane waited. He had no idea who Annie's new best friend might be. All he knew was when she left him she had been headed for Tajikistan.

"Think sports hero," Honor suggested.

Duane thought of Michael Jordan. Then he thought of Troy Aikman. Neither of them lived in Tajikistan, so far as he knew.

"Imran Khan," Honor said.

The name meant absolutely nothing to Duane.

"Is he a soccer player?"

"Cricket, you dummy—cricket! He's retired now, but in his time he was great."

Duane could not connect with Honor's information. As time passed he found it harder and harder to believe that he had ever been married to Annie Cameron at all. He had never seen a cricket match and had never heard of Imran Khan.

"Maybe they're just friends," he said.

"Could be," Honor said. "Though friendship is not the first thing you think of when you think of Imran."

"What would you think of me getting a vasectomy?" he asked.

"Because the lady of the moment doesn't want to have children, but is too lazy to worry about birth control?"

"That about sums it up," Duane admitted.

"Interesting," Honor said. "So the vasectomy was her idea?"

"I think it was mutual," Duane said.

75

Boyd cotton came back annoyed. Once again he had made a circle of the big pasture and saw neither Double Aught nor his track.

K.K. Slater was more than annoyed—she was crying.

"Sam just quit," she said. "He wants to go back to the Kalahari, or as close to the Kalahari as they'll allow him to live, nowadays.

"My main rhino keeps disappearing and my only San tracker wants to go home. I once thought this enterprise would work, but now I'm not so sure."

Myles came running over about that time with a cell phone pressed to his ear.

"They found him," he said. "He's in a town called Ralls."

"That's just this side of Lubbock," Duane said. "It's cotton country."

"He seems to have knocked over a school bus, but nobody was hurt," Myles said. "The bus was empty at the time."

"Come with me, Duane," K.K. said. "We'll fly out. There's room for you, Boyd, if you want to come."

"I don't," Boyd said.

"What about a flight plan?" Myles said.

"I don't think I'll bother with a flight plan. We'll just land when gravity pulls us down."

In less than an hour they were droning above the breaks of the Caprock.

It was nearly sundown—Duane himself had become a little anxious about where they might land.

Fortunately K.K. spotted a little crop duster's strip and eased the Cessna down.

The crop duster had just crawled out of his plane.

"Hear the news, there's a darn rhinoceros in Ralls."

"There better be," K.K. said.

76

WHEN THE FRIENDLY crop duster delivered them to Ralls, nearly a dozen patrol cars, various TV outlets and half a dozen cowboys were waiting for them. All the cowboys had their ropes at the ready, thinking it was their one chance to rope a rhino.

"So where is he then?" K.K. asked.

"Oh, he's right over . . ." one cowboy said, then nearly fell off his horse.

"He was right there," the local sheriff said. "Probably just slipped around behind the schoolhouse."

"I'll bet you a million dollars he's not behind the schoolhouse," K.K. said.

And he wasn't. Nothing was behind the schoolhouse except some basketball hoops with no nets.

Neither the cowboys nor the sheriff nor the local news outlets could accept it at first. They had seen Double Aught—he was there as big as life—until he wasn't.

"If you cowboys went to the trouble of taking your ropes down, why didn't some of you rope him?" K.K. asked.

The cowboys looked embarrassed and began, in ones and twos, to make wild, pointless dashes into the bleak neighbors of Ralls.

But all of them came back with nothing to show for their ardor.

"Oh boy, oh boy," the sheriff kept repeating.

The local embarrassment was so heavy that Duane couldn't bear it. He took a walk past the business district, hoping the great presence of the big animal would appear. But this time it didn't. No great presence rose out of the playgrounds of Ralls.

"Most embarrassing dern thing ever happened in Ralls," the sheriff said.

"Never mind, Sheriff—just never mind," K.K. said.

77

"**A**RE YOU UP to a night in this town?" K.K. asked Duane, when the sheriff finally desisted.

"What are my options?" he asked.

"Well, you could hitchhike home, if you just feel like deserting me," she said.

"No need to do that," he said. "Probably everyone ought to welcome the chance to spend the night in Ralls, Texas, once in their life."

There was a shabby motel nearby, a windburned place that catered mostly to the transient youth of the oil patch. Its rooms were not luxurious.

Fortunately there was a package store just across the street, where they were able to purchase a fifth of Wild Turkey. The motel called itself the Roughnecker's Lodge. The air conditioners in the rooms were stuttery, barely blunting the heat, so they each took a chair and sat outside, where they drank the whiskey out of very thin plastic glasses.

"What do you think of this Double Aught business, Duane?" K.K. asked.

"I got no theories," Duane admitted.

Actually he was more curious about K.K. and Boyd Cotton. When she hauled Boyd off to Seymour had they done anything other than eat a good steak? Somehow he doubted it.

"You're right that it's flat in this country," she said, watching the endless stream of trucks traveling east on Highway 82.

"We weighed Double Aught several times," she said. "He weighed nearly five thousand pounds, which means that he had a presence in time and space. Maybe this bad dream will pass and we'll find him in the morning."

"It's flat here, but the canyons off the Caprock aren't far," he said. "He could probably hide pretty well down in the breaks."

K.K. stood up and put her chair back in her room.

"'Night, Duane," she said.

Next morning the friendly crop duster rode with them as they hunted Double Aught in the breaks of the Caprock. They didn't find him. K.K. Slater looked more and more depressed.

78

DUANE PICKED A vasectomist out of the Yellow Pages. He first considered getting one in Fort Worth, so nobody in Thalia would find out, but then he decided that was cowardly, as well as inconvenient. He was a single man who had lived in Thalia almost all his life. People had talked about him when he was young, when he was middle-aged and now that he was old. His only real contribution to the life of Thalia was his entertainment value.

"That's right, it's your duty to have people talk about your vasectomy," Bobby Lee pointed out.

"Why?"

"Because there's nothing else to talk about," Bobby said, "and there won't be until football season comes around."

"Bobby, our football team hasn't won a game in three years," he mentioned. "Why talk about it?"

"That will change," Bobby Lee said. "Some team will come along someday that's worse than us and we'll win a game. Just have your vasectomy."

The doctor Duane chose, Dr. Jerome Germyn, was a bald man of about thirty who clearly did not like being bald. The evidence for this was the three hair transplants he had had, none of which had resulted in extensive hair.

One slicked-down implant was blond, another brunette, and a final one red and spiky, creating an unusual appearance, to say the least.

"You can ask about my hair," Dr. Germyn said. "Everybody wants to but mainly they manage to suppress their curiosity. Weird hair, or lack of it, is just something I've learned to live with."

Duane just shrugged.

"I expect you think I'm a little old to be worrying about this kind of thing," he said.

"Oh, no, not a bit," Dr. Germyn said. "Yesterday I snipped an old fellow who claimed to be ninety-one. His kids had grown up to be addicts and criminals. He just didn't want any more."

"Did he have a girlfriend?"

"You bet he had a girlfriend. He couldn't talk about anything else. His girlfriend was in her fifties but with these new fertility drugs anything can happen.

"This process takes about twenty minutes," he went on. "Then you need to go home and take it easy for a week. Wait about three weeks before you try sex. Your erectile function should be fine."

"What if it isn't—can I sue you?" Duane asked.

"Sure, if you want to feel like a fool in the courtroom. Most judges have problems of their own. They don't welcome lawsuits from old guys who can't manage to get a hard-on."

"I was joking, Doctor."

"My hair is really my problem," Dr. Germyn said, just before breaking into tears. His cry was violent but brief.

"Sorry," he said, when his tears subsided. "In my case hair is destiny. If I had abundant hair I might be a brain surgeon, instead of performing little snips on people who want sex but not babies. Of course, I might well have been a terrible brain surgeon. If you fuck up a vasectomy it's no big deal but if you fuck up brain surgery that's serious business."

Duane suddenly realized he didn't really want Dr. Germyn to do his vasectomy, but the realization came so late that he couldn't wiggle out of it. Dr Germyn did the snip, wrote him out a prescription and that was that.

79

DUANE DECIDED TO recuperate from his vasectomy at the big house, rather than the cabin. He felt a little queasy, as the doctor had said he might, but was otherwise okay.

He left Casey a message and then thought he might doze for a bit—then it turned out to be four hours, and when the phone woke him it was merely Dr. Germyn's assistant, asking if he was okay.

He left Casey another message, and then, idle, drove out to the Rhino Ranch, where Bobby Lee was fighting his migraines with a bottle of Stoli. He had finally adjusted to vodka.

Since he himself was the hero of a much more dramatic story—his penile implant—he could muster little interest in Duane's humble vasectomy. In fact his tone was so brusque that Duane felt a little ticked off.

"You may have a penile implant but I can't tell that you're using it much," he said. "Soon as I heal I plan to use my vasectomy night and day."

"Let's change the subject," Bobby Lee suggested. "You know old Boyd's out there somewhere. He thinks there's hanky-panky going on and he thinks it's only happening at night."

"Oh, meth you mean?"

"No," Bobby Lee said. "I think he's thinking about sabotage or something—hanky-panky her brothers might be doing."

"Boyd takes his Winchester and his .45 when he goes out," Bobby Lee said. "He's never done that before in his life, that I know of."

"Boyd's got pretty good judgment," Duane mentioned. "If he thinks he needs a saddle gun he probably does."

"Besides that the Texas Ranger's showing up tomorrow."

"Hondo Honda? Why?"

"I'm more or less the chief operating officer of this station, and yet I don't know why."

"At least you've got gainful employment, which is more than I can claim."

"By God, you're right," Bobby said.

80

THE MINUTE DUANE walked up to Casey Kincaid's apartment—or what had until recently *been* Casey's apartment, he knew what he was going to find: an empty apartment.

His brand-new vasectomy was not yet quite healed—it had been undertaken so that he might enjoy a pregnancy-free sex life with Casey Kincaid.

Standing outside her darkened apartment he realized that Casey had never really had the slightest intention of having normal sex with him.

He was so shocked by the magnitude of her deception that he had to grasp the handrail by the stairs for a moment; when he admitted to the truth—that Casey was gone—he was so shaken that he continued to hold the handrail tightly as he went back downstairs.

"Old," he told Bobby Lee, once the dreadful secret had been revealed They were on the tower.

"I'm old," Duane repeated.

"It ain't so much age as it is bad judgment," Bobby said.

"That's harshly put, Bobby—which doesn't mean it ain't true."

"Here come Dale and Roy," Bobby said, meaning K.K. and Texas Ranger Hondo Honda, who were loping in from their inspection tour.

"That damn fool can barely ride," Duane observed of Texas Ranger Hondo. "I'm surprised Boyd loaned him his second-best horse."

Just then the fax machine in the little office on the tower began to emit a fax.

"It'll be a sighting," Duane told him. "Somebody thinks they've seen Double Aught. Where is he this time?"

"Shiprock, New Mexico," Bobby Lee said, "I got laid there once."

Hondo Honda had his trademark rifle, with his trademark fringed scabbard. The two riders dismounted by the little corral. Boyd Cotton, who had been napping in his pickup, strolled over and reclaimed his second-best horse.

"Boyd's losing patience with this rhino business," Bobby Lee said. "He likes cowboying better."

"Who wouldn't?" Duane asked.

Bobby Lee looked at his friend.

"You ain't the kingpin anymore, Duane," he said. "I wouldn't be telling too many people about what happened with your vasectomy."

"I won't," Duane assured him.

81

About a month after Duane's surgery, Double Aught came back to the Rhino Ranch. Duane looked out the window of his house one evening and saw the rhino standing in his garden. He had done some damage to the greens, but had so far spared the cucumbers.

"Now you've messed up my garden—Dal may be right about you," he said.

He went back inside and called the local motel, where Hondo Honda happened to be staying while he investigated hanky-panky at Rhino Ranch.

"Hondo, the big boy is back," Duane said. "You might want to let K.K. know."

"I'll be right out, cowboy," Hondo said.

"I never cowboyed a day in my life," Duane reminded him.

"It's just a habit I got into and can't get out of," Hondo admitted. "I call far too many old boys cowboys, even though I know most of them couldn't find a cow in a week."

"Well, Boyd Cotton's still here, and he can find a cow anytime he needs to find one," Duane said.

Just then Duane saw Double Aught trot off toward the nearby highway.

"You'd better come, he's on the move," Duane said.

Hondo then hung up.

Years were to pass before the citizens of Thalia achieved any consensus as to what happened next. As with everything involving the black rhinos—as well as most things that happened in ordinary life—opinion in Thalia was often divided. Willy Moore, who had probably read more books than the fifteen hundred citizens of Thalia put together, said there was a book called *Seven Types of Ambiguity* and that if the critic ever visited Thalia he'd change his title to *Fifteen Hundred Types of Ambiguity*—but that was just a case of Willy parading his extensive reading.

There were only three eyewitnesses to what occurred on the road by Duane's house that evening: Duane himself, Texas Ranger Hondo Honda and a black rhino known as Double Aught.

Summonded by Duane, Hondo in his patrol car came smoking up the road a little too fast and when he sensed trouble coming hit his brakes and skidded to within a yard or two of Double Aught. It was dusk and the Ranger may not have seen the rhino too clearly, and, by the same token, the rhino may not have seen the patrol car too clearly, either. Nonetheless, the rhino concluded that he was under attack so he counterattacked, smashing the front windshield with his big horn. Then he backed up and made a run at the car, smashing in the driver's side door.

Duane knew by then that Hondo was in serious trouble, so he ran around to the passenger side of the car to try and pull him out.

Hondo seemed to be trying to get his Winchester out of its famed fringed scabbard, a line of action Duane tried to discourage.

"Forget your damn gun, crawl out the window and do it quick," Duane yelled.

The recommendation fell on deaf ears, because Double Aught started rolling the police car over and over, flipping it easily with his big horn.

Hondo took Duane's advice and stopped trying to free his rifle, at the same time firing wildly with his handgun.

Duane by this time had reversed his opinion: from his perspective Hondo was probably safer in the car than out.

Hondo shared that opinion: he gave up trying to get out but still fired off his handgun willy-nilly until the revolver was empty.

Soon the rhino rolled the patrol car into the middle of a fairly large highway. It seemed to Duane that he might have called Hondo into a situation that he might well not survive—he remembered being told by the small Asian woman Dal that Double Aught was not his friend. Nor, clearly, was he the friend of Ranger Honda.

Dal was right, Duane was pretty sure. Double Aught wasn't really any human's friend—and Dal had known this, although she had never seen Double Aught, who tired of his sport and went trotting off down the highway that led to the red light and the center of town. While Duane watched, he passed under the red light and passed on into the night.

And into legend. Despite thousands of sightings, Double Aught was never verifiably seen again.

This time Duane was glad to see him go.

83

HONDO HONDA EMERGED from his mushed patrol car with nothing worse than a skinned nose—or so it seemed at first.

Lights began to come on, up and down the route that Double Aught had taken after he tired of playing with Hondo's patrol car.

Soon crowds gathered around the patrol car and its semilegendary owner. Hondo was in the process of reloading his revolver.

"I don't know why you shot your own gun off six times," Duane said.

"Thought I might get lucky and kill the big son of a bitch," Hondo said.

Eventually nearly a hundred citizens gathered around to look at the mashed patrol car, and several truckers stopped to see what was going on. It was not long before Duane began to detect a negative current of opinion among the old ladies in their bathrobes and their husbands in shoulderless T-shirts.

The tone, Duane felt sure, spelled trouble for Rhino Enterprises.

"That big bastard ruint a perfectly good patrol car," one man said.

"Who told them they could bring these ugly suckers here anyway?" another asked.

"Whoa," Duane said. "The City Council voted unanimously to give all the help we can to Rhino Enterprises. You're on the City Council, Tom. I don't remember you abstaining, much less arguing against the measure."

"I was probably drunk and anyway who made you the big cheese, Duane?" Tom said.

"I'm not a big cheese but I am a citizen," Duane said. "Everybody I know was for the Rhino Ranch, including Bobby Lee Baxter—and as you all know Bobby Lee ain't for much."

Hondo happened to wander under a streetlight and Duane noticed something slick on his pants leg. On closer inspection the substance turned out to be blood.

But worse was to come. Duane saw what looked like the handle of a pocketknife protruding from Hondo's side, just below the hip.

Hondo Honda, who nearly always looked serene, lost his serene look when he saw the handle of his pocketknife protruding from his side.

"Maybe I better let you run me to the ER over in Wichita, cowboy," he said. "I was cleaning my fingernails when that call came and somehow I plumb forgot about the knife—I must have forgot to close the blade."

Just then Bobby Lee showed up in the company Range Rover. News of the commotion had reached the North Tower. Hondo was eased in the back seat, Duane with him—some lady had loaned them a towel to stop the bleeding with.

"Step on it, Bobby," Duane said.

Bobby stepped on it.

"I finally get a chance to see if these suckers will run a hundred and sixty, like they claim."

Nine minutes later Hondo was admitted to the ER in Wichita Falls.

"Five more minutes and this man wouldn't have made it," the young doctor said. "And he's not out of danger yet. Whom do we call if he starts slipping away?"

"K.K. Slater, I guess?" Duane said.

"Phone number?"

Both were stumped. Neither knew K.K. Slater's phone number.

"I can probably find it when we get back to the tower," Bobby said. "I work for the lady, I must have her phone number somewhere."

"Please give me something when you can," the doctor said.

"The patient probably knows it," Duane said. He scribbled down his own various phone numbers, and they left.

"I can't believe you let yourself get skunked by the likes of Casey Kincaid," Bobby Lee said, as they rode home at a sedate clip.

"I don't think I'm going to want to be talking about subjects like that for a while," Duane said.

"At least she was beautiful, you can't deny that," he added.

"If you don't smarten up where girls are concerned, your dick is never likely to rise again."

"It's none of your business," Duane said.

84

DUANE MET K.K. at the little company airstrip not much after dawn. Fortunately her phone number had been in the company computer. Hondo was still in the intensive care unit.

"I wish I could say he's critical but stable," the young doctor said. "But the truth is he's just critical. He's not out of the woods."

"No offense, but would a better hospital help his chances?" K.K. asked.

"Of course," the doctor said.

An hour later Hondo Honda was being medevaced to Methodist Hospital in Houston.

K.K. Slater cried when he was taken off and continued to drip tears throughout a difficult day.

The tears surprised Duane. He realized he had not quite understood her attachment to Ranger Honda.

K.K. picked up on Duane's puzzlement at once.

"I know, he's a figure of fun now," she said. "He's a caricature of himself—as Hemingway became. But there was greatness there once as there was with Hemingway."

"I see," Duane said.

"No, you really can't," K.K. said. "You would have to have seen him in his prime, when he was handsome as a god and everything a Texas Ranger ought to be. No thicket too thick, no bandit too fierce for Hondo to take on. He arrested half the drug lords along the border, at a time when our border with Mexico was one of the most dangerous places on earth.

"My father respected him," she added, "and he didn't respect just any old boy with a badge."

They drove for a while.

"Hondo was my first crush—I was maybe nine."

Then her voice broke and she sobbed openly for a while. Duane handed her a Kleenex.

"If he lives I'll take him to the ranch and make him head of security or something," she said. "I don't want him embarrassing himself like this."

"The townspeople are up in arms now," Duane informed her. "Double Aught rolled that patrol car almost fifty yards. Some of the old-timers are pretty hot—but that was coming anyway."

"Maybe I should call the PR people," she said.

"You can call them, but it won't do any good—in fact it will make matters worse."

"Why would it make them worse?"

"From the local point of view that would just mean more Yankees telling them what to do."

"Yankee—I'm not a Yankee and neither are the PR people!

"I can't believe what I'm hearing," she said. "After all that we've tried to do around here, the locals still think we're Yankees?"

"It doesn't matter where you're really from," he said. "If you ain't from here you're a Yankee, and that's that."

"What a fucking stupid mind-set," K.K. said.

"You're right about that," he said.

85

To make matters worse the large black rhino known as Double Aught trotted out of Thalia and rose into myth.

His treatment of the famous Texas Ranger Hondo Honda outraged the whole state. Gun shops between Amarillo and Laredo immediately sold out of high-caliber rifles. The hunt was on; but the hunt was fruitless. Several amateur hunters, while sighting in their rifles, had their shoulders broken by the recoil of the big guns.

Soon the state bristled with so many overpowered weapons that the governor had to issue an appeal for calm.

Hondo Honda recovered from his accidentally self-inflicted wound and joined in the appeal for calm. He even admitted that he had approached Double Aught too hastily.

"If you don't spook him I doubt he'd hurt a flea," he said.

Flea or no flea, many posses were organized and many hunts launched. All were in vain. Everybody expected Double Aught to reappear when the circumstances suited him.

"He'll come trotting up someday, like he always has," Bobby Lee said.

This time he was wrong.

Another shipment of sixteen rhinos was ready in Africa, but K.K. had the mission delayed. Something was weird at the Rhino but neither K.K. nor any of her experts knew what.

And, as Duane had predicted, the townspeople of Thalia convinced themselves that they had had enough.

86

DESPITE THE INCREASINGLY vociferous local opposition to the Rhino Ranch, K.K. Slater persisted. She brought the sixteen new rhinos in, and then another, smaller batch. Nearly sixty rhinos came to live on the rolling plains of Texas.

The City Council turned against K.K. but they proved to be the weaker entity. K.K. had a great ranch, and a billion dollars. She did not intend to be muscled aside.

Hondo Honda, gaunt now but still possessing his Winchester, came frequently and stood beside K.K. It being a dry year, several bulldozers were put to work, plowing fire guards. Bobby Lee was put in charge of security operations.

K.K. came so often that it set tongues wagging, mainly because she stayed at Duane's house when she came. Duane himself was often at his cabin during these visits, though he and K.K. usually ran into each other somewhere. The summer passed, then the fall, and still nothing had been seen of Double Aught.

Then the economy began to slide. Many of the expensive big game rifles were sold back to the gun shops where they had been purchased in the first place; though some of these shops were broke themselves, and soon found it necesary to close.

One day a major film producer came to K.K. with the idea of making a film called *The Legend of Double Aught*. In the film Double Aught would be an endearing old beast who was merely homesick for his home in Kenya. A major star would play a kindly shaman who arranged a spiritual transport of some kind: Double Aught would be whisked through the clouds back to his original home. A marketing plan was set in place—the major fast food chains would be filled with little rhino toys.

Unfortunately for the film, the producer was killed in a freak accident in New Mexico while he was participating in an illegal steer roping. He had been a cowboy star once and could actually rope—in this case fatally, when his horse fell on him.

From time to time Duane visited the offices of Moore Drilling. Once he happened by while Dal was not on her computer—on impulse he asked if she would go to dinner with him.

"There is no food in this town, Mr. Moore," Dal said, with a little smile.

"Hard to argue with that," Duane said. "I just thought I'd ask."

"I have not said no," Dal said, with her brief but delightful smile. "I want to eat with you. I am often lonely and I know you must often be lonely too. I want you to come to my room. If you allow me I will cook you a good meal."

"Consider yourself allowed," Duane said.

87

W HEN DAL ASKED Duane if he would like to have a meal in her room,
he assumed he meant in her apartment. But when he finally managed to find the place he discovered that it was only a room, and that it
was not in a nice or even safe part of town. Dal's salary was larger than
Annie's had been, and yet Annie's apartment had been in the best apartment building in town.

Dal's room contained a small table, a minute cooking range and a
pallet that must have been her bed.

"I am not strict," Dal said. "But it would be most proper if you remove
your shoes."

Duane had no problem with removing his shoes, but sitting cross-
legged, as Dal easily did, did not come easily. His joints were no longer
fully cooperative, but he slowly eased himself down.

"Are you all right, sir?" she asked, as she watched him awkwardly get down.

"I'm fine, and you don't have to call me sir," he said.

He saw that his remark vexed Dal a little—he saw something in her
gaze that surprised him.

"I said something wrong—I just don't know what."

Dal's look softened just a bit, as she put a bowl of very good-smelling
soup in front of him. Then she got herself a bowl and sat down.

"I must call you sir," she said. "You are older than my father, and I work
for your son. We Cambodians are a formal people, and much sorrow has
made us even more formal. We do not offer friendship quickly, and sometimes we never offer it, Mr. Moore."

"This is good soup, formal or not formal," he said.

"Yes, but you must not change the subject, sir," Dal said. "What two
people call one another is a serious matter, particularly a man and a woman. If we share correct matters someday we may be friends," Dal said.
"Then I can use your name, but for now I must call you sir."

Duane nodded. In fact he agreed. He had been casual in the wrong way.

Dal went on to feed him a delicious curry, the hottest he had ever eaten—in fact he could barely accept it.

"I can make it less hot," she said, but he shook his head.

"I want to eat it the way you eat it," Duane said.

"Okay, now I know."

After the excellent meal Duane asked Dal why she lived in the place she lived.

"It is what I can afford," she said, looking down.

Duane studied her. He didn't want to make any more mistakes.

"I thought Dickie paid you well," he said.

"He does, but I only keep a little," she told him. "I send most of the money home—I have a large family, many brothers and sisters, many nieces and nephews. Without what I send they would be very poor, and suffer very much."

Duane felt a fool. Of course he should have known that. Most of the illegals who worked for Moore Drilling did exactly the same. They sent most of their money home.

"I have good siblings," Dal said. "I am happy to help them and I would be unhappy if I didn't."

"Sorry, I should have figured that out," he said. "But even so I worry about your safety in this place."

Dal looked at him solemnly.

"I lived in Cambodia, sir," she said. "You do not need to worry about me."

88

For a few weeks, it seemed, America became obsessed with the disappearance of Double Aught. Bobby Lee, as manager of the tower, suffered the most aggravation from this obsession. Reporters, both from print and television, assembled almost daily to get an update on the news, which was no news. The big rhino was gone.

"If I'd known talking to the media was going to be part of my job, I'd have passed on the job," Bobby said.

"Maybe Double Aught fell in a sinkhole and got swallowed up," Duane mentioned. After all, sinkholes did occur. Moore Drilling had once lost a pickup to one.

"He weighs five thousand pounds," Bobby Lee said. "It would have to be a helluva sinkhole.

"The latest theory is mass hypnosis," Bobby Lee reported. "The people who sponsor it believe that Double Aught is the devil and he hypnotized America just to be mean."

Across the road a pickup stopped and some longhairs who once would have been called hippies set up a table and began to unload rhino souvenirs of various kinds.

"Who's that?" Duane asked.

"Some harmless little dope-heads," Bobby Lee said. "They sell rhino T-shirts and dozer caps and shit. They're polite enough and this is a country of free enterprise."

"I thought that was what K.K. planned to do for Rhino Enterprises?"

"Yep, but she don't seem to have got it off the ground," Bobby Lee said. "And if there could be a more boring job than the one I have it would be selling T-shirts and dozer caps beside a road almost no one ever travels, in a part of Texas most people would rather avoid."

They strolled down and introduced themselves to the young people, who were setting the table and propping up a shed. The young women looked to be about twenty-five—both were skinny, and their nipples were visible beneath their T-shirts—and were just the kind of women Bobby Lee had spent much of his life chasing.

One of the men—boys really—wore a mashed-up straw hat. The other, who was about to pump up some balloons, had lost a front tooth somewhere along the way, but seemed friendly.

"I'm Quentin," he said. "And this is Thomas, Belle and Jane."

"Howdy," Duane said. "Hoping to do some business selling balloons?"

"Sure, it beats working," Quentin said.

Then he looked at his companions a moment.

"We're not really interested in the rhinos," he said. "The truth is we're Satanists and all this shit we're selling is Satan-related. We're setting up here hoping the rhinos would bring a little extra traffic along this road."

"Satanists—I don't think I ever seen one even," Bobby Lee said.

"Well, now you've seen four," Jane told him brashly. "And you can take it or leave it."

"Oh, calm down, Jane—don't be rude to the locals, who happen to be neighbors," Quentin said. "And if they happen to be interested in the devil they're welcome to come to our church."

"You have a church of Satanism?" Duane asked, astonished.

"It's over in Olney," Thomas said. "It's modest at the moment—actually it's just my home. But we're hoping to get a building of our own pretty soon. Give them some literature, Belle."

"I been accused of being the devil plenty of times," Bobby Lee admitted. "But I never expected to run into somebody who actually worships him."

While they were chatting three pickups stopped. In no time Belle and Jane sold seven T-shirts with the devil on them.

"Bobby, they're not only here, they're doing business," Duane said.

"Makes you dizzy, don't it," Bobby Lee said. He found himself wondering if Jane had a boyfriend.

Duane knew the look on his friend's face.

"Are you getting ready to ask Jane for a date, or something?" Duane said.

"I could do worse," Bobby Lee said. "In fact I mostly have done worse."

89

"I HEAR YOU'RE DATING my replacement," Annie said, without preamble, early one morning.

"No, Dal doesn't date anybody," Duane told her. "She cooked me one meal, is all, and anyway I thought you were involved with some gentleman who plays cricket."

"That's over, such as it was," Annie said. "I'd like it better if you weren't dating my replacement."

"We're not dating," Duane insisted. "I figured you'd accuse me of dating K.K. Slater, who stays at my house pretty often when she's up here on business."

"I did hear that," Annie said. "I suppose both rumors could be true."

"Both are false," he said. "I did make a fool of myself, but that was with Casey Kincaid. But she shipped out for a busier place and since then I've just been batching."

"I probably shouldn't have divorced you," Annie said. "Despite some quirks you're nicer than most men. I wonder if it's final yet." Then she hung up.

Duane was inexpert at the new business of call indexing, though he made an effort. The number that finally came up was from the 310 area, which he knew was Los Angeles.

But when he called the number he got a message saying that the call was blocked.

What he *did* know was that he didn't want Annie back.

It was several months before she called again, by which time she seemed to have forgotten that he was nicer than most men.

1

"**D**AL'S TRYING TO persuade me to go to college," Duane said to Honor Carmichael, who was as silenced by the remark as he had been when Dal suggested it.

"I can barely spell," he said, as if that fact alone would render him ineligible for college.

"That's not much of an impediment," Honor said. "Just get a computer with spell-check on it. You'll have to acquire some computer literacy, of course, and the computer will help you with the spelling.

"So maybe your friend Dal is right. She's beginning to sound like a woman of substance, unlike your recent wife."

"Dal doesn't usually make suggestions unless they're good ones," Duane said.

"I'd like to meet her, next time I'm in Texas," Honor said.

"Why would you be in Texas?"

"Because my lover is in Houston, at M.D. Anderson—the cancer hospital."

"What kind of cancer?"

"Leukemia—the deadly kind," Honor said. "When she goes I might come and see you, like I did when Angie Cohen died. Except there won't be any sex this time."

Duane was silent.

"You *should* go to college, Duane," she said. "There's something called continuing education which is popular in colleges now. It's chiefly designed to stimulate older people—it teaches them stuff they've never had time to learn."

"What I never had time to learn would fill a barn," Duane said. "I was so busy being an oilman that I didn't even realize how little I knew. Whatever I've learned has mostly come after that day when I got out of my pickup and started walking."

"And you met me and I made you read Proust," Honor said. "I don't know how much you got out of it but it certainly couldn't have hurt you."

"What should I study?"

"Send me a curriculum and maybe I can advise you," she said. "And while we're waiting you might consult Dal."

"I think I'll do that," Duane said.

WHEN BOBBY LEE heard that Duane was planning to enroll in a continuing education program at Midwestern State University in Wichita Falls, he immediately became so angry and jealous that the tips of his ears turned red.

"All my life you've been lording it over me, Duane," he said. "And once you get a college degree you'll be fucking intolerable."

Neither Bobby Lee nor Boyd Cotton still worked for Rhino Enterprises. K.K. Slater severed her connection with the project. A team of South Africans arrived and did their best to turn the Rhino Ranch into an impressive game preserve.

They built three bungalows to live in, and eventually got the rhino population up to seventy-nine animals. They had as little to do with the people of Thalia as possible. Once in a while the South Africans would hit the country-western bars in Wichita Falls and pick fights with cowboys, roughnecks or airmen. Sometimes they won the fights and sometimes they didn't, but their effect on local affairs was minimal.

Bobby Lee had found a lucrative pumping job and had no regrets about leaving the Rhino Ranch.

Across the road the Satanists hung on for a while, but they didn't like the South Africans, who didn't like them, either, so eventually the Satanists moved to Olney, where they bought a small store and turned it into a church, near the air tractor factory. Other than the air tractor factory the two most newsworthy things in Olney were the Satanists and a one-arm dove hunt held every fall.

Efforts by the Baptists to run them out failed, as did a brief assault Bobby Lee made on the virtue of the young Satanist named Jane.

When Duane saw how upset Bobby Lee was by the news of his intention to go to college, he immediately asked Bobby Lee to go with him and take a few classes too.

"Go back to school? Me?" Bobby Lee said. He had not expected such a radical offer from his old friend Duane.

"Why not? If I can do it so can you," Duane said.

"Dern, that's nice of you, buddy," Bobby said, once he thought it over. He then blew his nose and seemed close to tears.

"We'll have to pick out our courses pretty soon," Duane said.

"Courses? Why can't we start with just one?" Bobby Lee wondered.

"Well, now that you mention it, just one might be a good idea."

"My brain feels tired already," Bobby said, at which point Duane thought he had better let the matter rest.

"I WENT TO THE Colorado School of Mines," Dal said. "I wanted to know what was in the earth, and now I do know. How was the curry?"

She was giving dinner to Duane and Bobby Lee at the tiny table in her room.

"It was the second hottest meal I ever ate," Bobby said. "And I lapped up every bite of it, ma'am."

"You don't have to call me ma'am," she said, with a mischievous look at Duane. He had never seen her look mischievous before.

"I am not Scarlett O'Hara," she added.

Neither Duane nor Bobby could immediately place Scarlett O'Hara.

"*Gone With the Wind*," Dal said. "Very popular in Asia. What have you eaten that is hotter than my curry?"

"There's a little Indian tribe in El Paso," Bobby explained. "They are the Tigua. They have a cafeteria that serves chili that's hotter than this curry. They say no whites can tolerate it. I didn't know that when I ordered the chili but I found it out pretty quick."

"The same would happen if you came to my village in Thailand," Dal said. "There they make a curry that it would not be wise for you to eat."

They had come to dinner at Dal's with the understanding that she would help them choose courses for the run they intended to make on college.

When news of their intention leaked out they were soon the laughing-stock of Thalia.

"Them two don't want an education," one wag said. "They just want a chance at young pussy."

Duane had secured a copy of the continuing education curriculum for the fall term and gave it to Dal, who glanced at it and handed it back.

"Do either of you like math?" she asked.

Both shook their heads decisively.

"There is a philosophy class that sounds just right for you," Dal said.

"Pre-Socratics to Wittgenstein," she said. "If you took it you could talk more intelligently with your grandson."

"Who would be a philosopher I might have heard of, other than Willy Moore?" Bobby asked.

"Of course there's Plato and Aristotle," Dal said. "Everybody knows about them."

"Well, nearly everybody," Duane qualified.

"I'm an oilman who barely finished high school," Duane said. "How would I know about old-timey folks?"

Dal had quit smiling. She was looking at them soberly—a look that carried some weight.

"I realize something that I didn't realize before," Dal said. "It is something sad, I'm afraid."

"You don't think we're smart enough to go to college?" Bobby Lee asked.

"Oh, you're smart enough—plenty smart enough," she said. "But you are not curious enough. That is the problem. If you are not curious enough and do not really want to learn then there is no reason for you to learn. You would just be a burden on the teacher."

Duane felt distressed. Now he had disappointed Dal.

"Maybe you're being too hasty," Duane said. "We've only had a day or two to get used to the notion that we could be students. Maybe we'll discover that we *are* curious about some of the things they teach in college."

Dal brightened at once.

"That is a possibility—thank you," she said. "I was too ready to accept defeat. I have had a hard life, with much defeat in it and I have come to expect it, I guess.

"I probably have some survivor's guilt," she added.

"What's that?" Bobby asked. "It sounds like the very thing I've suffered from all my life."

Dal looked at them both, thoughtfully.

"You should think about it a little," she said. "Maybe they do teach something you are curious about."

"I sure hope so," Duane said.

"I hope so too, boss," Dal said, wrinkling her nose in amusement.

D UANE GOT THROUGH to Willy on the third try. He sounded sleepy, but he listened as his grandfather mentioned that he might be enrolling in college, along with Bobby Lee.

"I have a hard time seeing either one of you in a classroom," Willy admitted. "But I think Dal may have had a good idea."

"So what about Plato and Aristotle?" Duane asked. "Do you think either of us could get interested in them?"

"Not a chance," Willy said. "I don't mean to be harsh but I don't think two old Greeks would really grab either one of you."

"Maybe we should give it up and just go on being rednecks," Duane said.

"I don't know—I'd like to meet Dal, but I'm going to Mount Athos during my break," Willy said. "One of the dons is taking three of us."

"What's Mount Athos?"

"It's the Holy Mountain in Greece— getting on it is hard. No hippies are welcome, so I'll have to cut my hair. But it might be worth it. Chances to visit the Holy Mountain are rare—I don't want to miss it. Some of the monasteries there have been there since the sixth century—imagine that."

"That doesn't mean I'll forget about you and Bobby," Willy said. "There must be something teachable you and Bobby could get interested in."

"I hope so," Duane said. "Dal will be disappointed if we don't."

L ATER IN THE DAY Duane and Bobby Lee decided to ponder the matter of their lack of curiosity from the restful security of a boat. They chose Lake Arrowhead for their pondering place. They put lines in the water but had little hope of catching much—it was not the croppie season.

"I wonder if they have a course in fishing, there at Midwestern," Bobby mentioned. "I bet I'd get an A if I took a course in fishing."

"Oh, there's lots of bass schools if that's all you want to try," Duane said. "Of course the slobs who teach bass fishing are even more ignorant than us. You're a record holder after all. You'd end up teaching them all your fine techniques.

"Willy left me a message saying we should think about literature," Duane went on.

"You mean like study Louis L'Amour?" Bobby asked.

"I looked through the curriculum and I didn't see his name," Duane said.

"Of course there's mysteries—I like Mike Hammer well enough."

"His name wasn't on the list, either."

"What kind of silly damn university, that they don't teach Mike Hammer or Louis L'Amour?"

"The kind that's the only one in driving distance," Duane reminded him. "I talked to Willy today and he said I should try to read a book called *Don Quixote*. He said Dal would probably agree."

"What's that one about?" Bobby Lee asked.

"Windmills, I think," Duane said.

DUANE AND BOBBY both felt a little uncomfortable going in the bookstore at the mall in Wichita Falls. Mainly their reading consisted of fishing and hunting magazines, and these were available at the Kwik-Sack in Thalia.

When they walked up to a counter and asked for a book called *Don Quixote*, the pert little salesgirl laughed at them.

"That's not how you say it—don't you guys know any Spanish?"

"Why would we, is this Mexico?" Bobby Lee said, though he knew it was a dumb answer—the Great Plains were filling up with Hispanics right before their eyes, and had been for some time.

"He didn't mean it—he knows there's lots of Hispanics here," Duane said.

"*Don Quixote* is not Mexican, it's Spanish and it's about an old crazy man and his friend, and was published in the early seventeenth century," the girl went on. She was quite pretty—Bobby Lee was happy to play ignorant to keep her interest though in fact he *was* ignorant.

"There are several translations—which do you prefer?"

"Just any one that's in English," Duane said.

"I wasn't going to give you one in Croatian," she said, and went and got the book, which was very thick, though, Duane thought, not as thick as Proust.

"You wouldn't think there could be this much to write about windmills," Bobby Lee said. "In my experience windmills are either working or they're broke."

"I hope we're not getting in over our heads," Duane said.

"I liked that girl at the counter," Bobby Lee said. "I wonder what her situation is?"

"Let's worry about *our* situation first," Duane said.

"MAYBE WE ARE just a little too old to be educated," Duane suggested, after he and Bobby Lee had been more or less stymied by *Don Quixote*. The prefatory matter quickly brought them to a halt. Neither had ever seen a book of chivalry and were none too clear about what chivalry was.

"Opening doors for ladies, I thought," Bobby Lee said.

"Maybe we can skip ahead and find the part about windmills," Duane said. "Windmills were in common use when we were younger, remember?"

"I know and they're trying to bring back wind chargers, but it don't help me read this boring book.

"I'm beginning to think I might just not be college material," he said. "Which was why I never went to college in the first place."

Duane was feeling much the same about himself. Try as he might, he could not get interested in *Don Quixote*, which was set so far back in time that he could find no way to connect with it. The famous incident of the windmills, when they finally found it, left them puzzled.

"Where's the mystery?—that old man is just crazy," Bobby said. "If he can't tell a giant from a windmill why should we read all this guck about him?"

"Nobody likes a person who gives up easy," Duane reminded him.

"I did notice that the peon had more sense than the old man," Bobby said. "Just like I got more sense than you."

"Maybe we could scan that list of college courses again—there might be something easier than literature," Duane suggested.

"It's just because you've got the hots for Dal—that's why we're doing this, ain't it?"

"I've got a poor record with women," Duane replied.

"*You've* got a poor record? What about me?" Bobby asked.

"What about evolution?" Duane asked. Scanning the curriculum he came to in the biology section and noticed evolution stuck in with the rest of the biology.

"Good lord, Duane," Bobby Lee said. "Most of the locals hate us anyway—how bad do you think they'd hate us if it got out that we think the Bible is lies and we all came from monkeys?"

"If evolution is that simple why would there need to be courses in it at a college?"

At that point the conversation lapsed, and so did their effort to read *Don Quixote*.

They were nervous about what Dal might think, but Dal, tactfully, held her peace, and, from time to time, continued to invite them over to eat her excellent food.

DESPITE THEIR DEFEAT by *Don Quixote*, Bobby Lee wasted no time in asking the perky salesgirl for a date.

"You have to remember I'm three years younger than you, Duane," Bobby Lee said. "It's why my sex drive is stronger than yours."

"That and the penile implant," Duane said.

"Best investment I ever made, by far," Bobby said.

"Sure. What better to invest in than your own dick?"

They were on their way to Possum Kingdom Lake, where Bobby Lee was hoping to break his own record with an even bigger bass.

"That girl at the bookshop's first name is Landry," Bobby Lee said. "She won't tell me her last name yet."

"I know Dal's last name but I can't pronounce it," Duane said. "I'm happy enough just to call her Dal."

He thought of Dal a lot and wanted to ask her out, but somehow she didn't seem like the dating type, and, anyway, as she herself had observed, there was no nice place to take her and certainly no place where the food would pass muster with someone who cooked as well as Dal.

Besides, Dal had a family in Asia. She had not mentioned a husband, but she was naturally reticent. There could be a husband, though somehow Duane doubted it.

In such a mood Possum Kingdom was perhaps the best place for both of them to be. He asked Bobby Lee to stop by his cabin so he could get his lure box, which took only a minute to snatch, but then, as they were leaving, the road leading back to the highway suddenly turned into a cloud of white dust.

"Who could that be?" Bobby asked.

"It could be Boyd Cotton, driving that herd of nilgai K.K. left behind when she got out of the rhino business," Duane said, and he was right. A piece of pasturage to the north had been purchased for the nilgai, which K.K. thought could be made commercially popular.

Boyd was not so much driving as he was leading the nilgai. Behind, in the dust, were the Hartman brothers, bringing up what strays attempted to oppose their removal.

"Hi, Boyd," Duane said. "How's the nilgai business?"

"Better than the rhino business," Boyd said. "We're thinking of expanding."

"We?"

"Me and K.K.," Boyd said. "I guess you heard that she's moving back to town. She's bought that old hotel and aims to fix it up and run things from it."

"Well, good," Duane said. "Things in these parts are just livelier when K.K.'s around.

"Any other news?" Duane asked.

"Nope—but I like working nilgai," Boyd said. "They're not as lively as cattle but at my age I probably couldn't handle too much lively," Boyd said.

"Are we going fishing or not?" Bobby Lee asked.

THE NEXT DAY Duane spotted K.K. on the roof of the old hotel. A horde of workmen were there and a big cement mixing truck was just backing up to the rear of the building.

"Hi, Duane," K.K. said. "I'm going to have a lap pool put on the roof of my hotel, which is going to look a lot different when I'm done with it."

"A which, you're going to have built?" Duane asked.

"A lap pool—it's just a narrow pool—you swim to one end and then swim back."

"Exercise, in other words," Duane said.

"That's right. Are you still walking?"

"I walk some," he said. "Why?"

"You look a little paunchy, that's why," K.K. said. "You should consider upping the walks. You're at the wrong age to let yourself go."

She looked at him in a friendly, if a sort of intense way. She asked about Willy and smiled when he told her Willy was in Oxford.

"I studied in Paris for two years," she said. "I studied some of that intense stuff Willy's studying."

Then she looked at him again.

"I think I know what's wrong with you," she said. "You've lost your sense of purpose. That happens to most of us at some point or another."

Duane was startled, mainly because he knew immediately that what K.K. said was true. A sense of purpose is exactly what he had lost.

"You're right," he said. "I don't feel necessary anymore.

"I guess the truth is I'm *not* necessary."

"You would be if I hired you to run the Rhino Ranch."

"I thought you was out of that."

"I gave the South Africans their chance but there's too much I don't like about their program," she said. "I think I'm going local again. What are you and Bobby Lee doing at the moment?"

"We kinda want to stay in college but it wouldn't be hard to talk us out of it," he said.

"Waste of time, maybe I can interest you in the Rhino Ranch again," she said.

A swarm of workmen were at work on what had been the old Mitchell Hotel and one of them caught her attention.

As he started to walk off K.K. grabbed his arm.

"I'm throwing a big feed tonight to announce my return," she said. "You and Bobby come. We've got a steer's head buried and we're cooking it in the old vaquero way, along with a couple of goats."

"What's the vaquero way?"

"We open the skull and eat the brains with some tortillas," she said. "Some sissies won't eat brains because of mad cow but I figure something else will get me first and brains, cooked right, are delicious—ask the French."

Far down the road from the south they spotted a car.

"Here comes my sweetie," K.K. said. "We got married, you know—don't you read the papers?"

"Not recently," he admitted. "You *married* Hondo?"

"Sure did—the billionairess and the Texas Ranger. Don't you even watch TV?"

"I thought he had a wife, Hondo," he said.

"Divorced," she said. She lives in Bullhead City now, in an elegant condo," K.K. said. "And I'm married to the man I've had a crush on since I was eight or nine."

She turned to address another workman and Duane hurried over to Bobby's pickup.

"Just drive, Bobby, and don't look to the right or left," he said.

"Why not?"

"'Cause you might see something you won't believe, and then you'll think the world's crazy," Duane said.

But his injunction came too late.

The Lincoln Town Car with Hondo Honda in it passed them. To their shock Hondo was sitting in the back seat, looking regal if still gaunt, and in front, driving, was a chauffeur in a suit and tie.

"You're right, I just seen something I don't believe," Bobby Lee said.

"I told you not to look," Duane said.

10

"**W**HAT IN THE goddamn hell do women want, anyway?" Bobby Lee asked. "A billion dollars and all she can find to marry is Hondo?"

"As to what women want, I would be the last to know," Duane admitted. "And you would probably be the next to last."

While they were debating what to do next Duane informed Bobby about their new job offer. He was opening his mail, at the time, and in his mail was a package from Willy. It proved to be a book, and was called *Animal Ghosts*. It was by a man named Elliott O'Donnell, and had been published in 1913. There was a brief note from Willy saying it might be useful in the matter of Double Aught's disappearance.

"I wish you hadn't even opened it in my pickup," Bobby Lee complained. "The last thing I need is some animal ghosts sneaking in on me."

"It could be a small ghost—a rabbit, maybe."

Duane scanned the book and soon discovered even elephants and gorillas would disappear, or appear, in ghostly form. Rhinos didn't seem to be mentioned, which didn't mean they couldn't become ghosts.

But the book only served as a brief diversion from the really big news of the day, which was that K.K. Slater had married Hondo Honda.

"I did notice that K.K.'s taken to doing a little bit more with her hair," Bobby said.

"Not much more," Duane said. In fact he had not noticed any difference in how K.K. did her hair, but he knew he was in the main just not sensitive to ladies' hairstyles.

"Of course a few women have married me," Bobby Lee observed. "From an outsider's point of view that might be considered just as odd as K.K. marrying Hondo."

"K.K. said Hondo was the real thing once—fought lots of bandits and rounded up lots of rustlers."

Bobby thought about that for a while.

"Lots of people become mere shadows of their former selves, I guess."

"Like who?"

"Well, like you, I guess."

"I'll be glad when we get to the lake," Duane said.

11

O N THIS STEAMY afternoon, destiny did not smile on the record-holding fisherman Bobby Lee Baxter. He caught a turtle and a gar.

Duane read the ghost animals book for a while before finally making a cast. He immediately caught a little bass.

"Nice, but not in the record class," Bobby Lee said.

Duane mentioned K.K.'s offer to make him manager of her considerably expanded operation.

"And you'd be my lazy overpaid number two," he added.

"When I was younger I didn't know I'd spend my whole life working for you," Bobby said.

"But you didn't spend your whole life doing anything of the sort," Duane reminded him. "You was manager for a while, as I recall, and it didn't particularly suit you. And besides that you ran a drilling company in Colorado for a while. You've had plenty of chances to boss, if that's what you'd rather do."

Bobby Lee was silent for a spell.

"I know that's all true, but it's like a dream in my mind," Bobby Lee said. "It was real, and yet it wasn't."

"Well, you cashed the paychecks—and you can keep on cashing them—bigger sums too."

"I guess that's what life boils down to, mainly," Bobby said. "Paychecks.

"At least that's a big part of it," he added.

"Sure enough," Duane said.

"**D**OING HER HAIR different, how different?" Honor wondered. She was more interested in K.K. Slater's new hairstyle than she was about her marriage to Hondo Honda.

"It's sort of more spiky now," Duane said.

"Okay, good choice," Honor said. "Are you in love with that Asian woman in the office?"

"Dal—no—she wouldn't want me in love with her."

"You don't have to have the woman's approval to fall in love," Honor said. "You either fall in love or you don't."

"Well, I haven't yet," he said.

"But you're fighting it, I'd say."

Duane realized sadly that his relationship with Honor Carmichael was dissipating in some measure. They had been too far apart, for too long— so long that they had become abstractions to one another.

"I wish you'd come visit," he said. "It's been more than a year."

Honor was silent for a while.

"I think I take your point," she said, finally. "We're slipping apart, aren't we?"

"That's how it feels," Duane said.

"Maybe I will come," Honor said. "I've those two sections of Daddy's land that I need to do something about."

"K.K. would probably buy it—she's in an expansion mode."

"Maybe, but Mike and Tommy have the first option," Honor said. "They've done so well with the deli that they want to retire and be cowboys."

"Well, we had a Bushman for a while," Duane mentioned. "Tommy was the only person who could really talk to him. Sri Lankan cowboys might work out just fine.

"Boyd could give 'em roping lessons," he added. "Maybe I'd even get him to give me roping lessons too. I need a hobby."

"I think I will come," Honor said. "I've become a little too Long Island."

"I don't know what that means."

"You don't need to," Honor said.

13

"**O**H GOOD," K.K. said, when Duane told him Honor might be visiting. "I've always wanted to meet her—we ran in something of the same circles once, but never managed to meet."

"Besides, Yves is due in tomorrow," K.K. said. "I do know that her girlfriend is something of a foodie, which probably means Honor knows her way around a soufflé.

"It can be a nice little test for Yves," she added.

"Who's Yves?"

"My new chef," K.K. said. "I don't think I can survive on the local staples anymore."

"He's not going to barbecue goats, is he?"

He actually liked goat, but had not found the steer's brains very appealing. He only took one bite, but noticed that K.K. ate it heartily.

"What kind of food is Yves planning to cook?"

"French food, of course," K.K. said. "Although maybe I should call it Mediterranean food. The fish will be almost as fresh as if you and Bobby caught it yourselves—all thanks to fast airplanes."

Duane had given the two bass he caught yesterday to K.K. and Hondo. The latter seemed to spend most of his day wandering around the rapidly evolving penthouse. He didn't actually carry the rifle in the fringed scabbard, but he kept it propped against a table where he could grab it quickly if the need arose.

"Hondo's not taking many chances," Duane observed. He still found the fact of K.K.'s marriage to Hondo a little difficult to believe. But he said it quietly—he already knew that K.K. would be fierce in defense of her man.

"I think I'm going to build an addition to this place," she said.

Duane thought she was kidding, but in the ensuing days truck after truck came up from the south, where K.K.'s stuff had been most of her life.

"I had forty-five rooms in the big house down south," she told Duane. "And mostly I had them to myself."

Soon trucks full of Scottish cattle, plus vaqueros to herd them, plus carpenters, hairdressers, laundresses, kitchen help of various kinds, poured into Thalia, and in many cases right on through it.

One evening near dusk Duane happened to look down the main street and saw lots and lots of the people of Thalia—to the extent that there were lots of them—standing under awnings or sitting under shade trees, watching what was clearly the beginnings of the transformation of their town.

Few of them had ever seen a chauffeur in a dark suit and tie sitting all day in a maroon Town Car, waiting to take people to the airport or bring people from it.

Not only had they never seen it, they had never expected to see it. Before their very eyes the crumbling Mitchell Hotel, a weather-beaten eyesore that the City Council had considered knocking down, before it fell down by itself and hurt somebody, was being turned into a palace, or something very like it.

Even as they watched, Duane from on high and the townspeople on their lawns or on their porches, *another* car, this one a limousine, stopped near the front of the hotel and disgorged a small, quick young man in a windbreaker, jeans and white tennis shoes. He had not shaved for a while—when he stepped out of the car and looked his new home over he looked dismayed.

"Uh-oh, it's Yves," K.K. said. "I better go down and smooth his passage a bit. I'm not sure he will immediately like what he sees."

"Immediately—why would he *ever* like it?" Duane asked.

K.K. ignored that question—at which point Hondo came and put his arm around K.K.

"Want me to go down with you, honey?" he asked.

"Nope, you've climbed those stairs enough for one day," K.K. said, giving his shoulder a pat, at which point Hondo at once sank into a lawn chair.

"Can you still shoot, Hondo?" Duane asked—he was surprised by his own question. What did it matter whether Hondo Honda could still shoot?

"Haven't been to the range in a while, cowboy," Hondo said. "I don't like to spend the money on ammunition, though I guess K.K.'s rich enough to buy me a bullet factory, if I was to need one."

There was a pause.

"Doubt I'll meet too many killers in this peaceful little town."

Then he yawned, and soon fell asleep.

Duane looked again at the townspeople of Thalia. He even gave them a halfhearted wave, but not a single soul waved back.

14

Honor had gotten heavy. She still had her beauty of feature, and her smile was delightful. But she had gotten heavy.

"I can see that you're shocked by my weight," she said, with a wry smile. Duane at once hugged her.

"It's been a while," he said.

"And during that while we've both grown old," she said.

In fact Duane *had* been shocked by Honor's appearance. He had blandly supposed she'd be slim and beautiful until she died. And he had supposed he would be mostly the same until *he* died.

But that was not the way of the world. He had seen the way of the world when he watched Hondo Honda creak around K.K. Slater's penthouse. Hondo was old, Honor was old and he himself was old. Hondo would never be mistaken for a vital man again—how lucky he was to have K.K. to take care of him.

What he experienced as he first looked at Honor had been shock—but once he had been with her a little while he began to see more of the old Honor in her movements and her laugh. She had, he knew, buried two lovers. He had buried one wife and lost another. No wonder she had changed.

"How do you feel about things?" he asked. He didn't know what else to say, right off the bat.

He sliced a couple of fresh tomatoes from his garden and grilled a pork chop—after she had flown from New York and driven from Dallas she might be hungry.

"I feel sad," Honor said. "I've loved and lived to bury two extraordinary Jewish princesses. They were spoiled to begin with and I happily spoiled them more."

"K.K. invited us to dinner," he mentioned. "She's hired this chef who just got here from Paris."

"Right, Yves Clair—she stole him from a very rich family—it's the talk of a certain set, just now. You don't steal other persons' chefs.

"Fortunately K.K. is richer than the family she stole Yves from. Liz wanted to hire him but I talked her out of it. In general stealing the help is bad form."

"He flew here from France and he's still just *help*?" Duane asked.

Honor nodded and ate her tomatoes.

15

"**I**'M SURE K.K. bought Yves an Aga stove and maybe accommodations for a live-in boyfriend," Honor said, as they strolled the few blocks from Duane's house to the Mitchell Hotel.

"What's an Aga?"

"A very good stove," Honor said. "*The* stove, in fact, for serious foodies."

"Okay, an Aga's a stove, but what's a foodie?"

Honor laughed—she had a rich, easy laugh.

"I keep forgetting how country you are," she said, putting her arm around him in a friendly way.

"A foodie is a cultivated person who's seriously interested in food and usually not too interested in anything else.

"And they eat at restaurants where chefs like Yves do the cooking," she added. "I know you told me when she first came here that she ate chicken-fried steak from the Dairy Queen, like everybody else, but that was just showing off. Besides which she had no real choice."

When they got to the hotel they saw that giant pots with tall cacti growing in them ringed the roof of what had very quickly become a penthouse.

"I bet those pots and those cacti weren't here this morning," Honor said. "One nice thing about the rich is that the trains run on time."

"Why do you look worried, Duane?" Honor asked, taking her arm off his shoulder.

"I *am* worried," Duane said. "What I know is that Thalia isn't interested in changing as much as K.K. wants it to change."

They saw Bobby Lee, sporting a clean white shirt and pressed jeans, come walking toward them. At least he had been invited to the dinner, which was a mark in K.K.'s favor, so far as Duane was concerned. Leaving Bobby Lee out would give Bobby a serious grievance, and he had plenty of those already.

"Don't worry, Duane—K.K.'s restless, like all rich people," Honor said. "In a few months she'll weary of her rural enterprise, and all those pots with all those cacti in them will simply disappear and K.K will move on to the next thing."

"Hope you're right," Duane said.

K.K. AND HONOR hit it off at once, as food the likes of which neither he nor Bobby Lee had ever seen poured out of the kitchen and was consumed: first there were snail's eggs, served on little pieces of toast. Then came a pile of raw sirloin seasoned with various spices. This, he learned, was steak tartare, followed by a cold soup and then a fish baked in thin pastry.

Hondo Honda was served a different menu: a minute steak and French fries. He drank two glasses of wine and slowly nodded off—finally his head slumped on his chest.

K.K. went on chattering with Honor.

"I know this is impolite, guys," she said. "Honor and I seem to have to talk through the whole Social List, which is great fun for us but no fun for anybody else."

"It's like being an English boy and not going to Eton," Honor said. "Eton's great for those who go there but it irritates the hell out of those who don't."

"I have a grandson who's a Rhodes Scholar," Duane reminded them. "When Willy gets home I guess he can hold forth with you two better than I can."

"That's for sure," K.K. said.

Honor looked at Duane solemnly for a moment.

"Willy will always be someone to be proud of," she said. "And he'll always be your grandson. But I don't know that he'll ever be home."

"Willy escaped, and the rest of you didn't," she said.

K.K. Slater looked down and said nothing.

17

THE DINNER PROGRESSED at a measured pace. K.K. and Honor talked about ski resorts and private islands—then they talked about fashion designers—odd, to Duane's ear, since K.K. never wore anything but khakis. Then they talked about affairs people they knew might be having, or might not be having.

Their chatter was casual and friendly—good cowboys getting together after a branding might talk in much the same way, though not about the same matters.

Still, Duane found himself getting uneasy. Once, when he had gone to relieve himself, he happened to glance over the pots full of cacti, down toward the Kwik-Sack. Six or eight people were gathered—two or three teenagers, a couple of roughnecks and old Mrs. Banner in her wheelchair—she lived next door to the Kwik-Sack and relied for entertainment on what was happening in the parking lot. Now she was just one of the onlookers who were staring at the penthouse of the former Mitchell Hotel.

The sight of those folks, all of whom he knew, made Duane deeply uneasy. He couldn't really say *why* he felt so troubled—but troubled was how he felt.

Dessert consisted of several sorbets, followed by coffee and brandy. K.K. and Honor each drank a little brandy but Duane passed. Bobby Lee took one sip and became even more silent than he had been up to then.

When they got up to leave Duane saw that the crowd in the parking lot of the Kwik-Sack had grown. There were maybe twenty-five people there, and what was wrong with the picture was that he ought to have been one of the crowd at the Kwik-Sack, not one of the people eating snail's eggs and drinking brandy on K.K. Slater's penthouse with Honor Carmichael.

When the dinner ended and they walked home they came within hailing distance of the Kwik-Sack. Some of the roughnecks had left but Mrs. Banner and the kids were still there. The people in the crowd were still as statues. Nobody waved—Duane couldn't blame them. How friendly was it to eat a meal that cost at least a thousand dollars in front of people who mostly fed themselves out of a microwave?

Honor wobbled a little—it was the brandy. When they got to Duane's house she went straight to bed, in the room K.K. usually stayed in.

Duane couldn't sleep. He knew he wasn't going to take K.K.'s offer and become her manager—it just didn't appeal.

Maybe Bobby Lee would take it—but Duane didn't really think so—and if he took it, it wouldn't be for long.

He had no real explanation of his own attitude. Some things were okay to do in Thalia and some things weren't.

18

"**K**.K. wanted me to be her overall manager but it just wouldn't work," Duane told Honor the next morning.

"She mentioned it while you were in the gents'," Honor said. "She was hoping I'd persuade you."

Duane shook his head.

"Half the people in this town hate my guts already, just because I'm prosperous," he told her. "I worked pretty hard for forty years in order to *get* prosperous, but the crowd at the Kwik-Sack don't remember that."

"Some of them are too young to know it, Duane," Honor said.

"True," Duane said. "But if I start ordering the townfolks around I'll soon be in real trouble."

Honor had showered and was wrapped in one of Duane's bathrobes.

"I think you're in real trouble anyway," she said. "But the trouble you're in is with yourself. Certain levels of luxury bother you, right?"

"I guess they do," he said.

"Well, there's really nothing wrong in flying a fish, or a chef, from Europe, if you've got the money," she said. "K.K. has the money.

"There's nothing *bad* about serving snail's eggs," she went on. "It's just boring. The bronzino was good, though, didn't you think—that fish in the pastry shell?"

"It was good," Duane admitted. "But Bobby Lee and I could have caught her something just as tasty not twenty miles from here."

Honor looked at him silently for a moment.

"You're right—you certainly shouldn't take K.K.'s job. You've got a class problem. I think I'll jump in the pool and take a quick swim, if you don't mind."

"Help yourself."

"Actually I did notice it, when I was your shrink," she said, when she came back from her swim. "But that was the least of your problems then

186

and I don't remember addressing it. Of course at that time Angie was probably the only member of the upper class you'd ever seen, and except when we raided your garden you didn't see much of her."

"What about you?"

"Me—come on. I'm just a middle-class girl from Vernon, Texas."

"Well," Duane said.

"Well what?"

"What about your girlfriends? If you spend your whole life, nearly, with upper-class girlfriends, don't that make you upper-class—I don't really know what upper-class is."

"I think you're right, honey," Honor said. "I sort of snuck into the upper class by fucking. Perceptive of you to see it.

"Of course I am well educated," she added.

Duane said nothing.

B OBBY LEE TOOK the news of their nonemployment hard.

"No big salary," he said.

"It's me that's out of work," Duane said. "For all I know she'd still be happy to hire you."

"Not in a month of Sundays, she wouldn't," Bobby Lee said. "I'm just a workingman."

"So am I," Duane reminded him. "I was the boss for a while but if I worked for K.K. I wouldn't be the boss."

Bobby Lee thought about it.

"Well, she did hire me once," he mentioned. "She hired me and Boyd and after us it all went downhill."

"I think she'll not only hire you again, this time it'll be for more money.

"Besides I think one other person has turned her down, and that's Boyd. He says he can get all the work he wants being arena director at these little rodeos around here.

"It's not exactly cowboying, but it's pretty close," Duane said.

"Actually K.K.'s the bossiest person I've ever met," Bobby Lee said. "She should just stay around and do the bossing herself.

"And mind Hondo—that old Ranger is fading fast."

"Yes, and it may be that we've been unfair to the man," Duane said. "He had a big reputation once—I 'spect he must have done something to deserve it. But that doesn't explain K.K. marrying him just as he was fading out."

"Maybe that shrink in your guest room could explain it," Bobby said.

"I don't know—at one time Honor helped me get back to my right self, more or less. But she doesn't exactly *explain* things—she just describes them in a smart way."

"She got you to read that book that I can't get through ten pages of,"

Bobby Lee reminded him. "And she got you to go to Egypt, and you're not exactly what I'd call a traveling man."

After that, conversation lapsed, but two days later Bobby Lee was once again head security adviser at the Rhino Ranch. He got a bit of a raise, to boot, but there was one little drawback: he had to wear a uniform, and it itched.

Honor Carmichael drove off alone and made her land deal with Mike and Tommy, giving them two scrubby sections just north of their deli. Soon it was overrun with scrawny yearlings purchased for them by a cattle buyer with a big appetite for Asian-style barbecued pork.

That night Honor and Duane went to dinner again at the penthouse of what had been the old Mitchell Hotel. This time Yves had secured some crayfish (crawdads to the locals) and also some Kobe beef. Duane had eaten Kobe beef several times before: Annie Cameron had approved of it and served it now and then in their home in Arizona. What he didn't agree was that it was somehow better than well-fattened Texas beef.

"I agree with that," K.K. said. "But I'm breaking Yves in here and I think I should let him cook what he's familiar with for a while. He'll come around to local produce—all the good chefs do—but right now he doesn't know what the local produce is, or where to find it."

"Give him time," she said.

"You should start up your garden again," Honor said. "Then Yves would have all the local produce he needs."

"What garden?" K.K. asked.

"It's one I planted as a memorial to my wife the year she got killed."

"He's too modest—it was a world-class garden," Honor assured her. "It was nearly an acre and it was free to the public too. Poor people could come as often as they wanted to."

"Maybe I will start it up again," Duane said. "Though it's a little too late for this year."

On the walk home Duane didn't look toward the Kwik-Sack. He didn't want to know who was there.

21

THE NEXT MORNING, having decided once again that walking would be his primary mode of locomotion, he strode briskly off toward the post office.

On his way he happened to see a small dejected man sitting on the curb near where the old theater had been. The small man was smoking, but slowly and wearily. He was unshaven, with at least a three-day growth of stubble.

The small man was Yves, the chef.

"Hello," Duane said, to be polite.

"Hi," Yves said.

Duane walked on, got his mail and returned. Yves was still sitting there. He still smoked, and he still looked unhappy.

"Hungry?" Duane asked.

Yves looked surprised.

"Why yes, I am hungry," Yves said.

"I live four blocks down the street," Duane said. "Be happy to cook you breakfast. There won't be any snail's eggs, but my neighbor keeps chickens and I can probably snitch an egg or two and we can scramble them up.

"And I've got some pretty good German sausage, from the little German community down the road. Don't know if they'll meet your standard."

Yves smiled, for the first time.

"I'm licking my lips," he said, in perfect English. "Anything you don't have to fly in sounds good to me."

He got up and the two strolled along the empty street to Duane's house.

Out of his chef's uniform Duane found the chef to be a friendly young man.

"Where do you hail from?" he asked.

"L.A., but I've lived all over," Yves said.

191

He watched carefully as Duane scrambled four large brown eggs, added a tomato and some good onions, and offered Yves a beer to wash it down with.

"Good," Yves said when he had cleaned his plate. "Thank you for rescuing me from the hell of post–Chez Panisse-ism."

"Before breakfast you didn't look too happy," Duane remarked.

"She fired me," Yves said. "I was better off cooking for that old queen I was cooking for on the Riviera. I don't think she means to chauffeur me back to the airport, either. I guess I need a taxi—does this town have a taxi?"

"No, but don't worry—I'm a man of leisure and I have two daughters that live fairly close to that airport. I can drop you off and visit my daughters.

"Now my grandson would insist on hitchhiking, but you look like you could use a ride."

Yves grinned. "I'm pretty good at hitchhiking myself—I really don't want to put you out."

"It wouldn't be putting me out—it'd be giving me something to do," Duane said.

"And we might even be able to eat a little North Fort Worth barbecue on the way," he added.

"Deal," Yves said. "Let's go. I've got my passport and enough money to get me anywhere in the world. If we go back to the hotel that old Texas Ranger might shoot me."

"He wouldn't do that, but she might," Duane said.

"Should we wash dishes?"

"I think the dishes can wait," Duane said. "I don't know K.K. very well but I think she might be about to get her dander up."

"It's up," Yves said. "I'll treat you to the barbecue. That was a perfect breakfast."

22

"I cooked on k.k.'s ranch a few times," Yves confided, as they were finishing the ribs and brisket in a dim eatery in North Fort Worth.

"It was like feeding dinosaurs," he said.

"Thanks," Yves said again, when Duane dropped him at Terminal C at D/FW. "If Thalia was your town instead of K.K.'s I might have learned to like it."

"Only natives really thrive in Thalia—if anybody thrives," Duane said, and drove off.

He rethought his initial resolution to go visit his daughters, and just went home. He was old and his daughters just middle-aged. Why not train them to come see him? After all, their idol K.K. Slater lived there, though, somehow, K.K. had not bothered to invite either of them to her penthouse dinners.

Probably she just didn't consider them weighty enough in financial-social terms to bother with except in the most limited way.

"Don't ever forget something about the very rich—there's an aspect they share with the very poor," Honor told him once.

She looked at him to see if he wanted to guess, but he didn't.

He waited.

"They're mean," she said. "They're bred to unrealistic expectations, which in high and low alike provokes bad behavior. Hemingway discovered how mean Alice B. Toklas was to Gertrude Stein, but no one ever discovered how mean Angie and Liz were to me."

He reflected on the comment as he drove home, changing highways at the last minute so as to visit Moore Drilling's offices in Wichita Falls. He was hoping Dal might be free, but she wasn't free and he felt silly waiting, when it was clear that he had no reason to be there except to chat with her.

When he left he decided to stop by the Asia Wonder Deli and have a spring roll or two. To his surprise Tommy had a cast on his arm.

"What happened to you?"

"Tommy very bad cowboy," Mike informed him. "Fall off his horse twelve times."

"And only broke one arm?"

"Didn't break it falling," Tommy said. "Horse kick me and that's how this arm broke."

Boyd Cotton walked in in time to hear that part of the conversation.

"He got too close to that sorrel filly of mine," he said.

"How's it coming with the Scottish cattle you're supposed to be handling?" Duane asked.

"I never thought I'd see a quadruped dumber than the nilgai, or more boring; but that was before I tried Scottish cattle," Boyd said. "They're fine cattle, but they are just plain reluctant to move. Whatever place they find themselves stopped at is good enough for them. They can eat all the grass right down to the roots and they still won't move."

"Does K.K. ever come around?" Duane asked.

"Not if she can help it and particularly not if she knows I'm there."

"That surprises me," Duane said. "I thought you were the one person around here K.K. fully approved of."

"That was true at first," Boyd acknowledged. "But then she noticed my independent attitude, and our relations suffered a change."

"How'd you know that your independent attitude was the problem?" Duane asked.

Boyd just looked at him, and secured himself a little more pork barbecue.

"I withdraw the question," Duane said. "I helped one of her slaves escape this morning. She may not care for my attitude that much."

Later, driving home, Duane began to feel sorry for having spoken harshly of K.K. Slater. Boyd Cotton, whom K.K. clearly respected, had been rather harsh also. But why? K.K. had not done anything bad to either of them. If there was anyone in the North Texas projects she *didn't* treat as help, it would surely be Boyd, and after Boyd, himself.

She was no more to blame for being born rich than the watchers in the Kwik-Sack parking lot were for being born poor, or being brought up ignorant.

At least K.K. hadn't heard them being harsh—it was some consolation, but not much.

23

F EELING VERY MUCH at loose ends Duane drove home. As he was walking to his back door he heard sounds from the pool and went to see what was what. To his surprise K.K. Slater was the swimmer. She was swimming purposely the length of the pool time after time. She wore goggles and a bathing cap. When she saw Duane she swam to the edge of the pool and ripped off her bathing cap.

"I hate bathing caps," she said. "It's not as if my hair was anything to write home about anyway."

Duane had supposed K.K. might be annoyed with him for having spirited away Yves but she wasn't.

"It was nice of you to take the little diva to the airport," she said, climbing out of the pool. She wore an old-fashioned, one-piece bathing suit.

"He didn't seem like he was going to make the adjustment to North Texas life."

"It doesn't seem like I am, either," K.K. said. "My lap pool leaked, which is why I took a chance and borrowed your pool. I've been spoiled by my own help—I mean my native South Texas help. I have a lap pool at home and it's never leaked. One virtue I can't claim is patience. I want things to work like they're supposed to work, damnit!

"Is that too much to ask?" she said.

"Yes," Duane said.

K.K. stared at him for a moment and then agreed.

"You're right—nothing's perfect on this planet," she said, "though Boyd Cotton's number-one quarter horse comes pretty close.

"Do you have even a spark of sexual interest in me?" she asked.

"K.K., I'm so far over the hill that I can't remember what the hill felt like," he said.

"Hondo and I have what the French call a *mariage blanc*," she said. "I suppose the whole town knows that. The old boy's ridden his last ride, if you want to be nice about it.

"When Hondo was young he saved my father's life twice in desperate situations—that border has always been wild," she said. "I promised Daddy I'd always look after Hondo, and I have. His balls are in his abdomen, you know."

Duane was stunned. "They're where?" he asked.

K.K. seemed unaware that her news was a kind of bombshell.

"I don't know the whole story, but Hondo got a bad disease in Mexico once, which meant that his balls had to be stitched into his abdomen. Fortunately he had already sired his family by then."

She gathered up her towels and got ready to depart.

"Use the pool anytime," Duane said.

"I will, but I still want my damn lap pool to stop leaking," she said.

BOBBY LEE BAXTER, who had had both testicular cancer, losing one ball in the process, and also a daring penile implant that he liked to talk about when he could find anyone who would listen, was riveted by the news of Hondo Honda's problem.

"I've heard of that disease—it's one reason I stay out of Old Mexico," he said. "They say your balls get as big as grapefruits."

"But, Bobby, there's hormones now—if you was to lose your other ball you get by on hormones and probably do fine."

"Hormones might make me grow tits," Bobby said.

"Could you imagine me with tits?" he asked.

"Even if I could I'd rather not," Duane admitted.

"It was you brought up Hondo and his problems," Bobby reminded him.

"Yes, and I bitterly regret it," Duane said.

25

U NDER PRESSURE FROM virtually everyone he knew, Duane finally broke down and got a cell phone, one of those with a little holster that he could clip to his belt.

The first person to call him on it was the person who had called him most often, over the years: Bobby Lee Baxter.

"I didn't believe you'd really answer," Bobby Lee said. "I consider you the last holdout, and now you ain't held out."

"You're no one to talk—you were the first person I knew to get a cell phone."

"Yeah but I was in the hunt, and you wasn't," Bobby said.

"I still like phone booths better, but there's very damn few left," Duane said. "The cell phone's killed the phone booth."

"Be old-fashioned if you want to," Bobby said. "I've gotten quite a few pieces of ass thanks to the cell phone."

"How many?" Duane asked. He was determined to pin his friend down.

"At least two," Bobby claimed.

Duane unclipped his cell phone and its holster and put it on the table in the cabin, where he had been spending a lot of time.

It was three days before the cell phone rang and when it did ring it was Dal.

"Mr. Moore, are you feeling bad?" she asked.

"Not particularly, but then I've been at the cabin for three days."

"Our computers are down," Dal said. "They are down all over Texas. I thought of you and was thinking we could go eat at that place run by those weird Sri Lankans—if you would like to. They say the computers will be down for three hours—so we would have time."

"I would just love to," Duane said. "I hoped to talk to you the other day but you were too busy."

"I know—I knew you needed me but I had to do my job," she said. "I had to pay attention to the sands.

"I would like to help you now, if it is not too late," she said.

"Thank you," Duane said. "It is not too late."

26

THEY AGREED TO meet at the Asia Wonder Deli. Duane got there first but Dal soon arrived driving one of the company's pickups—an old one, much dented. She drove with confidence, though, and was wearing a conical hat to protect herself from the fierce sun.

At the deli she first ordered tea, smiling at Mike, who liked her.

Duane asked for iced tea, which caused Dal to wrinkle her nose.

"Tea is drunk all over the world," she said. "Most places it is served hot, which brings out the flavor. Yet you Texans drink it iced. I don't know why."

"I was raised drinking it cold," Duane said. "I was grown before I knew about hot tea."

They secured one of the tiny tables and Mike and Tommy plied Dal with their finest delicacies.

"Are those rhinos still around?" Dal asked.

"They're around but they try to keep them away from the roads," Duane said.

"It was a mistake to bring those animals here," Dal said, very firmly. "The sooner they are all dead the better."

"Well, the whole point of bringing them here was to keep them from being all dead, which I guess would happen pretty soon if we'd left them in Africa."

"If I were free and did not need to work I would take you as far from those animals as I could," she said. "I felt yesterday, when I was working, that you needed me. Many would need me if I let them, but since my husband was killed I have pushed away these men who need me. But I don't want to push you away. I want to help you in my modest way."

"You have helped me," he said. "You have.

"And I'd like to help you too—I'd like for Dickie to provide you with a better pickup, for one thing."

Dal put her hand on his.

"This is not about pickups, Mr. Moore," she said. "Yesterday when I was busy I felt you pulling at me. You didn't interrupt, but I felt you pulling anyway. But today the computers are down. I can try to help."

"Would you live with me?" Duane asked, to his own surprise. "You could have your own wing of the house. This wouldn't involve sex, if you didn't need it to. I know how hard you work, but we could eat together, maybe. Of course if you had to work late I'd understand. I've worked late a lot, myself."

There was a pause. Dal looked at him a long time, but pleasantly. But she did not make an immediate reply to his request.

"I see now," she said. "I didn't know you were so lonely."

Just then her cell phone rang—it was Dickie.

"They're coming up," he said. "The computers, I mean?"

Dal immediately rose.

"Think about it—and I'm going to see that you get a better pickup."

"No—I like my little beat-up pickup," Dal said. "You men always focus on the wrong things."

She squeezed his hand though, and then left, leaving his question unanswered.

When he thought back on the conversation it embarrassed him a little that he had asked a woman he barely knew to live with him. And yet she had not been offended by the request. Once he was alone again he realized that Dal had called one thing right. He was lonely. When he got back to the big house he watched the Tennis Channel for a while—and he was still lonely.

Once he had had enough of tennis—the U.S. Open was on—he walked out in his garden to get a tomato. He stood for a while, enjoying the starlight. When he got back to his kitchen he noticed that his message light was blinking. The message was from Dal and asked him to call her as soon as he could.

"I am a late-hours person," she said in her message. "You won't wake me."

Duane called her back immediately.

"Howdy," he said, a little nervously.

"Oh, now you play the cowboy," Dal said lightly. "You are no more a cowboy than those silly Sri Lankans—I think they are probably Bangladeshis anyway. They work too hard to be Sri Lankans. I think they called themselves Sri Lankans because it sounds more Oriental. And who would know?"

"Well, not me," Duane said.

"I see you have a hard time coming to the point," she said. "You asked me to live with you and I accept. I can come tonight, if you wish. I have very little—just my few clothes. So, yes or no, should I come?"

"Yes," he said. "Come but be careful on the roads."

"Dickie will not be very happy with my decision," she said. "I will need a few computer hookups—will you ask him to do that for me?"

"I sure will—I doubt he'll mind."

"You are wrong about that," Dal said. "But I don't think he'll fire me—I make him too much money."

"He won't fire you, I'll see to that," Duane said. "I still have some influence with the company."

"You don't have much," Dal said.

Duane thought about it and realized Dal was probably right. He hung up and went back outside. The night was brilliantly starlit.

In thirty minutes Dal in the beat-up pickup swung into his driveway. Duane helped her carry her few things into his house.

She inspected her room—it had once been the master bedroom and she seemed to like it.

"Plenty of wall space to put in the computers," she said. "Thank you for this—now we are buddies, right?"

"Right."

"This way neither of us will be quite so lonely," she said, and closed her door.

28

THE NEXT MORNING Dal left early—before first light—Duane had just walked out to his garden, intending to do some weeding. Dal gave a friendly toot on her horn and was gone.

He had a saddle shed and a little pasture west of his house—the small pasture was about ten acres. At the moment he was allowing Hondo Honda to leave his aging quarter horse there, since it was in easy walking distance of the Mitchell Hotel where Hondo lived.

Dal's taillights were just a red spot in the distance when Hondo himself came striding along. He moved a good deal more briskly than he had been moving lately. In five minutes he had caught his horse and saddled up. Duane had slept poorly—the dramatic move he and Dal had just made was much on his mind. So far Dal and Hondo both were outperforming him.

Hondo had lifted the horse's left front leg and was giving the hoof a critical examination.

"Need to get this old pony shod pretty soon," Hondo said.

"What brings you out so early?" Duane asked.

"Just felt like a trot," Hondo said. "K.K.'s off to Dallas, to one of them dern meetings.

"Said she'd be back for supper," he added.

He started out of the driveway and then turned once more to Duane.

"Tell her not to worry none about her Texas Ranger," he said. "She'll always be my little bride."

Then he trotted off down the highway toward the Rhino Ranch.

To Duane's mind Hondo looked snappier than he had ever looked. He stood watching, quietly surprised as the sun lifted above the horizon.

Pretty soon Bobby Lee's pickup appeared, headed in the other direction from Hondo. When their trajectories narrowed for a second Bobby

Lee waved at Hondo and Hondo waved at him. Duane stood and waited until Bobby Lee pulled up.

"Hondo's looking chipper, for a change," Duane observed.

"It could be good eating and regular sex," Bobby Lee suggested.

"Somehow I doubt it's regular sex," Duane said.

He told Bobby about Dal moving in.

"I hope Dickie won't be too upset," Duane said.

"Dickie would only mind if it affected Dal's work and it won't," Bobby said. "Your girls will have a fit though.

"They won't want a gook sleepin' in their mama's bed."

"Their mother's bed was sold ten years ago, at least," Duane reminded him. "Other people lived in the house for a while. They both know that."

Just then Bobby Lee's cell phone rang. He contemplated ignoring it, and then answered. After all a rhino might be on a rampage. The Hartman brothers were once again his backup squad, and it was one of them who called.

"He *what*—no way!" he said, profoundly shocked.

"What?" Duane asked.

"Hondo just hung himself, that's what. Climbed to the top of the tower, tied a rope to a pipe, put his head in the noose and jumped."

"And nobody tried to stop him?" Duane said, deeply shocked himself.

"Dub or Bub stop a Texas Ranger?" Bobby said. "That'll be the day."

Duane got in the pickup and they raced to the North Tower, where, sure enough, Hondo Honda was hanging from a rope. The drop had almost torn his head off. His rifle, in its scabbard, lay on the ground below him.

Pickups full of oilfield workers or cowboys began to stop—several already lined the roads.

"He dropped his rifle—he'd hate that if he knew it," Bobby Lee said.

THE TEXAS RANGER known as Hondo Honda, whose real name was George Brody, was buried with some ceremony in the cemetery of his hometown of Cuero, in South Texas. At the last minute it was decided not to bury his famous scabbarded rifle with him—it was given, instead, to the Texas Ranger Hall of Fame, in Waco. The Hall of Fame got his pistol too. All that went into the coffin with him were his spurs and his Texas Ranger badge.

K.K. Slater, his bride of a few weeks, flew her own plane to the funeral. She asked Duane to come. She plainly was grieving, so he went to support her.

Sixteen serving Texas Rangers were at the funeral. The governor had meant to attend, but chucked at the last minute. An aide came and read a special commendation from the governor and the state legislature. Hondo's old quarter horse had been brought to Cuero, and was formally unsaddled for the last time—K.K. was putting him out to pasture once he had played his part in the historic funeral. Hondo's first wife had not been able to make it but his three sons were there, all looking uncomfortable in their suits.

There was talk of a twenty-one-gun salute, but with only sixteen Rangers able to make it that plan was abandoned.

K.K. and Duane were driven back to the tiny airport by one of the Rangers.

"As a courtesty to you I won't start getting drunk until we land," she said to Duane.

There were tears on her cheeks.

"Not much of a record, for me," she said. "I marry for the first time at fifty-two and my husband hangs himself a month later."

"Just before he rode off he said you were his 'little bride,'" Duane told her.

"Hondo loved clichés, as you may have noticed," she said. "Nevertheless I'll mourn him forever. When he was young he was the most handsome man in the world, and the bravest."

In a little while they landed, flying out of a red sunset that made the whole plain seem fiery.

Bobby Lee met them and drove them into town. Duane mentioned to K.K. that Dal had moved in to live with him as a companion.

K.K. looked startled—Duane realized that she had probably never met Dal, or even heard of her. She was one of many workers.

If K.K. felt personally slighted by the news she didn't show it. When she asked where Dal was from he said Cambodia.

"Dickie works her hard," he added.

"I wonder why you have such a thing for these young analysts," she said.

"Dal's not real young," he said. "She's in her forties, somewhere."

"However old she is your daughters are going to hate it," she said.

Then she went into the hotel where she lived.

"See, I told you," Bobby Lee said.

"Well, if it's a problem, it's my problem," Duane said.

THE TROUBLE CAME in a phone call, both sisters on the line. Nellie was the most irate. Julie had a tendency to sulk during crises.

"She only wants your money, Daddy, otherwise she wouldn't be sleeping with an old man like you," Nellie said, not quietly. "She's just a little gold digger like Annie Cameron."

"Thanks for the compliment," Duane said. "In the first place Annie Cameron was richer than all of us put together. She has her problems but she doesn't need to gold-dig.

"Beside which," he went on, "Dal makes extremely good money. She doesn't need to gold-dig, either.

"And in the third place Dal and I are *not* lovers, but we're both old enough to need a little quiet companionship now and then."

"Baloney," Julie said. "Why would you bring her here unless you wanted to fuck her?"

"I didn't bring her here, Dickie did—and I have to say I don't like your tone."

"I don't want her sleeping in our mother's bed," Nellie said.

"Be hard for her to do that since your mother's bed got sold more than ten years ago."

There was silence on the line.

"And I particularly don't like it that you're talking trash about a decent woman you've never met."

"We're just trying to protect you, Daddy," Julie said. "You've always been a kind of a sucker when it comes to women."

"And that includes your mother?"

"You all were real young then," Nellie said.

"Keep in mind that I *asked* her to move in and I didn't do it immediately," he said. "The fact is I *need* her, not as a lover but as a friend. And I have to say I'm very disappointed in both of you. I'd like it better if you were at least mannerly."

"This isn't about manners, Daddy," Julie said.

"Everything is about manners, Julie," he said. "And until both of you grow up and apologize I don't want to see either one of you around here."

"Well," Nellie said, in a shocked tone.

"I mean it," Duane said, and hung up.

31

THE NEWS THAT Duane Moore had banished his daughters from his big house spread through Thalia in maybe an hour. It might be that the news traveled faster because neither of the Moore girls had ever been popular. Even as little girls they were judged to be snooty. Marrying rich urban husbands didn't improve matters, even when both of the marriages failed. One of the girls became a nun, briefly; the other became a lesbian, also briefly. The few who bothered to assign blame for the girls' snotty behavior blamed Karla, their mother, now dead many years.

"That Karla, she was a wild one—should have paid more attention to those kids," was a comment frequently heard. It was heard at the bank, the filling station, the post office or the Kwik-Sack, the normal channels through which public opinion flowed, as it had all Duane's life.

When Dal learned that Duane had banished his daughters, mainly on her account, she seemed to take it in stride.

"In their minds I have taken their father," she said. "I am not surprised that they resent me.

"Still, they do not seem very grown-up," she added.

"That's the problem, they're not."

"I like living with you," Dal said. "But maybe it was a mistake."

"It was no mistake—we get along, don't we? I suggested it. I want to live with you."

They were having tea—hot—on his deck. It was well after sundown, but the redwood planks were still hot from the day's sun.

"I think Annie Cameron wants you back," Dal said. "She is very jealous of me. She thinks everything should be hers."

"That's right," he said. "She thinks everything should be hers—while she wants it, that is."

"Life is not consistent, Duane," Dal said—she had finally dropped the "Mr. Moore."

She got up to put the teapot back on the counter when Duane's phone rang.

"Fucking her yet?" Annie asked.

"You're as rude as my daughters," he said.

"Well, she's got my husband and she's got my job," Annie said. "Don't mind if I am rude."

"You left your husband and you quit your job," he reminded her. "And these things happened long before Dal arrived. I'm going to tell you what I told my daughters—leave me alone if you can't be more polite."

"You didn't answer my question—are you fucking her yet?"

Duane hung up.

K.K. USUALLY ASKED Duane to breakfast at her penthouse. Dal would long since have been at work. She left his house at three-fifteen and was hard at work by three-thirty.

K.K. frequently made breakfast herself, usually steak and eggs and hash browns, with Duane contributing a couple of tomatoes.

Duane enjoyed his breakfasts with K.K., and it was not lost on the citizens of Thalia that he was breakfasting with one woman and dining with another.

Often he and K.K. sat together, looking off to the horizons, under a bright clear sky.

"I ought to get back to work but I can't get Hondo off my mind—poor man."

"Karla just died in a simple accident but I was a long time getting over her—if I have," he said.

"I've had a skimpy sex life and now here I am fifty-two," K.K. said. "I'm not particularly good-looking but I am very rich."

"Is that much of a help?"

"Means I could buy a stud," she said. "But I never seem to get around to it."

"There's probably an answer but I don't know it," he said.

"I hear the people think you have an Asian mistress," she said.

"Dal leaves at three-fifteen and gets home about eight," he told her. "Wouldn't leave much time for screwing, even if we were lovers, which we're not."

"I may go to Africa tomorrow," she said. "I miss Africa. You'll have to make your own breakfast for a while."

"Back to batching, I guess," Duane said. "I'll miss your company."

"Why not go with me?"

Duane shook his head.

"Spoil sport," she said.

"**M**Y MOM'S FREAKING OUT, as you probably know, Grandpa," Willy said, long-distance from Oxford. "She's trying to use me to sway you—an old tactic."

"Right," Duane said. "I cut them off until they can be polite to Dal, who is a nice woman, and one who's had a much harder life than your mother and your aunt."

"I bet she's not even your mistress," Willy said.

"Nope. So how are you?"

"I wish I knew more math," Willy said. "My German's coming along but I sure don't have enough math."

"What's the big thing you need math for?"

"I'm beginning to think you need math for everything," Willy said. "In honor of Einstein I've been rowing lately. Being on the water is very relaxing. Einstein and his wife rowed on a lake called Lake Listerine—it was given to Princeton by the man who invented Listerine."

"They still got the benefit of some exercise, I guess," Duane said. "Do you like it over in England?"

"Love it," Willy said. "I feel like I'm in a civilization at last."

"Any plans to come home?"

"Not immediately. On my next break I'm going to France to see the cave paintings. When Picasso saw them he said the cave painters had done everything, which is quite a compliment."

"I'll take your word for it," Duane said.

"Why did that old Texas Ranger hang himself from the tower?" Willy asked.

"If I could answer questions like that I'd be rich enough to build some genius a lake like Einstein had."

"Come on, what would you call it?"

"Why not Lake Willy?" Duane asked.

"That would really freak my mom out," Willy said. "I think you should call it something else."

"How about Lake Geritol, then?"

"Why not Lake Moore? It would please my mom and Aunt Nellie."

"Nope, can't—people would think I was putting on airs," Duane said.

SOMETIMES DAL WOULD have to work late—Duane would begin to miss her before she got home. Sometimes he waited in his driveway, waiting to see her headlights swim onto his road.

He had come to think of his house as their house but Dal didn't think of it that way. She used the kitchen to make them tea or a simple meal, but she had scarcely been in the rest of the house—just her bedroom and bath. She had never been in Duane's bedroom.

On some nights, when Dal was late, Duane would drive out to the North Tower—it was still the only tower that had been built—and visit with Bobby Lee for an hour. Bobby Lee was being paid lavishly, and was the only person in Thalia, other than Duane, who seemed to enjoy K.K.'s confidence.

Most of the activity Bobby and his deputies observed was meth cooking, as it had been from the beginning. Bobby Lee reported every fire, resulting in the arrests of many meth cookers, and yet the volume of infractions did not decline. There was an animus in the meth community against Bobby Lee, and yet he came to no harm.

The possibility that he might worried Duane though.

"I hope you keep that rifle loaded," he said, referring to the weapon propped against a cot.

"*That* rifle? That rifle was meant to stop a charging elephant or rhino," Bobby Lee said. "The kick would probably kill me. I've got a pistol, and Boyd Cotton's Winchester. Meth heads are crazy but not real smart. I could probably hold them off with my light weaponry."

The words were scarcely out of his mouth when a pickup with hugely oversized tires came bouncing across the cattle guard and headed for the tower.

"I think they mean to ram us," Duane said, picking up the big game rifle as a precaution.

"Let 'em," Bobby Lee said. "This tower is set in reinforced concrete. That rig there is just meant for car shows."

The big rig nudged the tower once or twice but did not attempt to push it over. Two men got out, one skinny and one a well-known local bodybuilder named Lewis. He wore a T-shirt that said KICK ASS.

The other man was Donald Deek, the bad seed of a family from Dundee, population not many.

Duane and Bobby had known both men for much of their lives—neither of them was likable. Lewis was a skilled bow hunter who was not careful about whose deer or turkeys he shot.

"If you're looking to buy a rhinoceros you've come to the wrong place," Bobby Lee said. "All ours are spoken for."

"Fuck you, Bobby—we don't want no rhino," Lewis said. "We want you to stop calling the fuzz every time we decide to cook a little meth."

"Most of whose ingredients are legal anyway," Donald Deek said.

"Right, it's just the combination that's illegal," Bobby reminded them. "Besides which, this is grass fire country. I don't care if you bathe in meth, I just don't want you setting fires in a tinderbox year like this."

"I'll climb up there if I have to and throw your skinny ass half way to Olney, if you don't stop it," Lewis said.

Duane had employed Lewis several times over the years—he was fairly good help on a rig floor. He walked over and looked down at the two men. Donald Deek was one of several dealers who had supplied Dickie during his addict years.

"I think you men best go home," he said.

"Nobody asked your opinion, Mr. Moore," Deek said.

"However that may be, I'm standing with Bobby," Duane said. Then he went over and picked up the big game rifle he had recommended earlier.

"Just stop calling the fuzz, that's all we want," Lewis said.

Duane chambered a shell into the big gun, set the gun firmly against his shoulder and blew out one of the pickup's oversized tires.

The two meth cookers were stunned. Their pickup sagged badly to one side.

Duane ejected the shell and put the rifle back where it had been before. The kick had indeed rocked him back on his heels.

"I hope I didn't dislocate my shoulder," he told Bobby. "I think you better stick to guns you aren't afraid to fire."

Both Deek and Lewis were on their cell phones. Both turned out to be calling Triple A, which, soon enough, came to their rescue.

That he had won the dispute did not reassure Duane, or Bobby Lee, either.

"Other than ruining a big tire, and maybe dislocating my shoulder, that accomplished nothing," Duane remarked. "They were just the leaders, not the troops."

By way of answer Bobby Lee pointed north, where a tiny but bright flame shone; a meth fire, obviously.

It angered Duane.

"We should have climbed down and stomped their asses," he said.

Bobby Lee smiled.

"If I was you I'd take a good-sized club if I meant to subdue Lewis," he said. "Nobody ever said Lewis was smart, but he is stout."

Duane was calming a little.

"And you're old," Bobby Lee reminded him.

"No getting around it," Duane said.

35

FROM THAT NIGHT ON, the meth wars accelerated in Thalia County. A few days after the encounter at the tower fourteen fires were set, three of them on land Moore Drilling owned north of a little creek called Middlefork. And the other fires were not far away. It was trash casually thrown in Middlefork Creek that had caused Duane to launch his personal crusade against litter.

A new sheriff had just been elected in Thalia County, a woman named Lena Loftis. She was the first woman sheriff in the neighborhood and her election had only been made possible by the gross misbehavior on the part of the previous sheriff, who had taken forty-five minutes to answer a drive-by robbery at the Kwik-Sack, two blocks from his office.

Lena Loftis was a big stout woman who had grown up on a hay farm and could toss one-hundred-pound bales of hay onto the hay wagon as well as any man.

Duane liked Lena and voted for her. When her victory was confirmed many of the good old boys in town announced that they were moving away rather than accept the indignity of acknowledging the legitimacy of a woman sheriff.

Despite much vociferous talk, in the end not a single good old boy moved away, except for old Tom Lawton, who only moved into his grave.

Lena Loftis let Duane ride with her when they inspected the fires on his own or his company's property. There were five fires and no meth heads at any of them.

"They're taunting you," Lena concluded. "They set these fires and then cook the meth in their bathtubs, I'd guess."

"I don't much like how things are looking, Sheriff," Duane said. "We're lucky it's a calm day. If it was a little more windy we'd be calling in the fire trucks now."

Sheriff Lena got a fire extinguisher out of her trunk and killed what was left of the fire.

Duane happened to look to the north—he had been looking south as he helped douse the fire. When he did happen to look to the north he noticed a bright flame he had not seen before. It was his cabin, and it was burning.

"Uh-oh," Lena said, when she saw what had caught his attention.

"Those little fuckers!" she added.

"One of them isn't little," Duane said.

36

A FIRE TRUCK SOON CAME from the nearby hamlet of Holliday. There was little they could do—mainly just wet down the smoldering embers. Duane's cabin was gone.

"We'll get them on arson, now," Sheriff Lena said. "Maybe put them in the Big House for a while."

"I don't think it was Lewis and Deek," Duane said. "They're too lazy to produce something on this level."

"What level?" Lena asked. "It was just a plank cabin, right?"

"Right, but it takes thinking about and I doubt those two can think that well," he said.

The more he walked around the smoking embers the more convinced he was that the two meth heads were not the arsonist. The little fires, yes; but the cabin, no.

The moment his shift ended Bobby Lee came over, filled with outrage and ready to go after Lewis and Deek.

"It wasn't them," Duane said. Sheriff Lena had gone back to town, but suggested to Bobby that he go give Duane a ride.

"It wasn't?" Bobby asked.

"I don't think so—I don't think they'd have the balls," Duane said. "Besides they both worked for us once. They might have at least a smidgin of loyalty—knowing they might need to work for us again."

"But they're meth heads, Duane," Bobby reminded him

"When the coals cool down I'll go through them with a rake and see what I find," Duane said.

"What would you be looking for? You never kept much but a change of shirts and some fishing gear in this cabin, as I recall."

"One thing I had was that book Annie gave me: *Desert Solitaire,*" Duane said. "It's hard to burn a book up. If it's there I'll find some trace."

"What are you driving at, Duane?"

"Annie gave me that book, and she's not one to leave much behind," Duane said. "I bet she came back and took her book."

"And set the fire?" Bobby had never liked Annie.

"And set the fire. That would be my guess."

"You're right up there with me when it comes to finding mean women," Bobby remarked.

"Dal isn't mean," Duane said.

"Well, she's Asian," Bobby Lee said.

DUANE CAME BACK the next day with a rake. Some of the embers were still smoking. He found a burned-up frying pan and a few charred kitchen utensils, but no book.

Now that he had had time to think he realized Annie had never meant to give him the book, anyway.

"It's a first edition and it's signed by Ed," she told him. "He gave it to me himself. Don't set a coffee cup or anything down on it."

Duane was careful to keep the book protected. He put it on a high shelf by his bed. Apart from a few fishing magazines it was the only reading matter in the house. He would have been the first to admit that he was not a reader.

He didn't think the book would have been wholly consumed but he could not find a trace of it in the embers, not even a flake or two. He knew, when he thought about it, that Annie had come back, taken her book and burned down the cabin.

"Why'd you burn me out?" he asked, but to himself.

Then he put the rake back in his pickup and drove to his hometown.

"**O**F COURSE SHE did it and the motive is not far to seek," Honor said. "The motive is revenge."

"But she left me."

"Yes, but you let her go—you didn't fight to get her back."

"Oh," he said. "You think that's what she wanted?"

"Sure. Where's the fun in adultery if the wronged partner doesn't seem to care?"

"She was halfway around the world," he reminded her.

"But there are airplanes that would have taken you there. Maybe you were a little relieved when she dumped you. She can't have been easy to live with."

"Why would it have been a relief?"

"Well, there was the sexual problem, for one thing," Honor said. "Pressure to perform."

"Oh," he said.

"The cabin was a part of you she couldn't have. Women don't like that. Can you blame them?"

"Sometimes I can't tell whose side you're on," he told her.

"My side, of course," Honor said.

THREE DAYS LATER, after Duane had already arranged to have a new cabin built on the old spot, Lena Loftis showed up at his house early one morning and handed Duane his missing book.

"Found it in a crack house south of town," she said. She had taken the precaution of putting the book in a Ziploc bag—it seemed to be unblemished. The whole scenario about Annie burning the cabin down and reclaiming the book was obviously wrong.

"Thanks, Sheriff, I feel like a fool," he said.

"You may have been wrong about your former wife's involvement, but the fact remains that your cabin got torched," she said.

"Maybe a rat chewed a wire," he suggested.

"And maybe a meth head torched it," the sheriff said. "Do you ever see that old rhino you used to see?"

"Not since the night he smashed up Hondo's patrol car," Duane said. "I don't believe there've even been any sightings since that night.

"Once in a while there will be a sighting but they never pan out. One I even heard on talk radio came from Greenland. Greenland!

"I don't think we'll see Double Aught again," Duane said. "But twelve more rhinos are coming this week, according to K.K.

"I don't think K.K. realizes it but there's a lot of anti-rhino sentiment building up in this town—and a good deal of anti-K.K. sentiment too.

"Frankly, it's never been that welcoming a place," Duane said. "I suspect there's even some negative feelings about you. Being the first woman sheriff can't be all gravy."

"I can handle it," Lena said. "Guess what, though: the city now wants to put up a statue to Hondo Honda. They think it would bring in tourists."

"A statue to Hondo—he barely lived here ten days."

"They still think it would bring in tourists."

"I thought that was what the Rhino Ranch was supposed to do?"

"Besides that they don't like it that you're living with a gook—their word, not mine. I've barely seen the lady but she seems real mannerly."

"They like Asian cooking so much that they've made ranchers of Mike and Tommy, and they object to Dal?"

"You know these folks better than I do, Mr. Moore," Lena said. "They're deeply prejudiced but not so prejudiced that they can't tell good food from bad."

"It's a case of food overcoming prejudice, then?"

"That's how I read it," Sheriff Lena said.

40

Toward the end of summer Dal went to Thailand for a month, to see her children and grandchildren. Her parents were dead.

Her absence wore on Duane a good bit. They were not lovers, but he missed her more than he might have Karla, Honor, Annie. At night he slept little. He felt vulnerable to attack. He took to sleeping with a revolver on his bed, something he had never done in his life.

There were so many meth addicts in the county that virtually anything they could lift and carry became prey. Theft of oilfield equipment was rife. Some of the big equipment—bulldozers and pulling machines—were taken south into Mexico.

A few were recovered at the border, but most were never seen again.

Without Dal, Duane became so jumpy and irritable that Bobby Lee, for one, could scarcely endure his company, and told him so.

"If you need her that much, marry her, Duane," he said. Often the two of them got drunk on the platform of the North Tower. Bobby was now allowed to ditch the uniform.

Duane had often thought about marrying Dal, but it was an area that was not settled in his mind.

"I might, but I doubt she'd have me," he said.

"It can't hurt to ask."

"Well, it might," Duane said.

DUANE HAD BEEN counting the days until Dal returned. Three days before she was due to arrive Dickie called and told his father she would be a few days late.

"But why?" he asked.

"Well, she routed herself through Munich, and if she's in Munich she might as well go through Geneva and meet a few people there—it's just business."

His father didn't answer, but he did have a sad look on his face. It made Dickie wonder if maybe things had gone farther between Dal and his father than he had supposed. They had been housemates for a good many months—it would be natural enough for them to become lovers.

It was a development that Dickie would welcome—though his sisters certainly wouldn't.

Dickie saw what the girls might have missed—that their father was getting older and might really need a wife to look after him. Often Dickie would find his father sitting in a lawn chair outside the big house, looking lonely. Except for Bobby Lee he had no cronies. Marrying Dal might be his salvation, keep him lively for several more years.

Right now it was clear that he was disturbed to hear that she would be delayed three days—a mere three days.

Duane was disappointed but not entirely crushed. He adjusted. The oil business was global—if Dal and Dickie felt there was a good business reason for her to stop through Geneva, then they were probably right and he should get over it.

One way to soothe himself would be to go fishing, which he promptly did.

K.K. SLATER WENT to Africa and returned no worse for wear. The update on Double Aught was negative but she seemed not to care, particularly. And she had brought a new chef with her—or perhaps just a cook. Duane had never been exactly clear about the difference.

Stephanie Slade was long-legged and somewhat horsey, with big front teeth and very long brown hair. She wore cutoffs and T-shirts and, on her first evening, cooked Duane and K.K. a delicious gumbo. Her legs, like so many girls', were nicely tanned.

"I think Steph might stay for a while," K.K. said. "She's from Plano—she won't have to deal with quite so much culture shock."

"I don't know about that, K.K.," the girl said. "Where's my North Park Mall?"

"Steph wants to open a cooking school," K.K. said.

"Oh, please—not a cooking school: a culinary institute," Stephanie protested.

"And then you'll run off with a busboy," K.K. predicted.

"Could happen," Stephanie admitted. "I do like the guys."

To Duane's surprise K.K. had already pledged a good amount of money toward the statue of Hondo Honda. She had even, herself, commissioned the artist, a highly thought of sculptor from Colorado. His name was Colby Jordan.

"Highly thought of in the world of Western art," Stephanie insisted.

"I know you despise it," K.K. said, amiably. "We'll see how it goes when Colby actually gets here."

"Yuck, I met him, he's bowlegged and has a big old turnipy schnozz."

"And he tried to fuck you?"

"Of course," Stephanie said, blushing a little.

"I could have made this hotter," she said, sampling her own gumbo.

Just then an egg-sized rock came flying out of the darkness and hit the table between K.K. and Duane, shattering a wineglass and just missing Stephanie.

"Hey, what the fuck?" she said.

Duane hurried to the edge of the building but saw no one. Below him the red light blinked on and on.

The courthouse lawn, across the street, was empty.

"Hey, they chipped my table," K K. said. The table was of polished mesquite.

"This is not good," she added.

"It isn't," Duane said.

"I just gave the town a lot of money to put up a statue of Hondo—maybe I ought to shut that down. Why would they throw rocks at me?"

"Well, for one thing, it's a mean, miserable little oil patch town," Duane said. "Strangers nearly always wear out their welcome, no matter how nice they try to be."

"I'm not so sure I'm going to like this job," Stephanie Slade said.

Duane continued to watch the street below them, hoping the kids—if it *was* kids—would show themselves and give him the finger. Chunking unwelcome strangers was not an unheard of practice in Thalia. He himself as a teenager had probably done it once or twice.

K.K. Slater said nothing more.

43

THE NEXT MORNING Duane put the rock in a baggie and showed it to Lena Loftis. The sheriff operated out of a small office in the old, shabby Municipal Building. Sheriff Lena worked in a kind of stall. A lot of Post-its were stuck to the wall behind her desk.

"Where does Deputy Dub sit when he's around?" Duane asked.

"In his car," Lena said. "Dub's so big that when he comes in he has a tendency to sort of steam up the place.

"Dub's got a good heart, though," she said, "which is more than I can say for Bub. They may be twins biologically but they sure ain't twins in temperament."

"You think Bub might throw a rock at K.K. Slater's penthouse?"

"Sure, and he's got the arm for it too," Lena said. "When he played catcher for the baseball team he tried to pick someone off at second and the ball sailed so high it hit the center fielder in the head."

"I wonder if there could be fingerprints on this rock," Duane asked.

"I don't know but we've had Bub's prints on file since he was about nine, when he began to break and enter," the sheriff said. "He was the cat burglar of Thalia."

"I'd like it tested, if it can be," Duane said.

"Any teenager in town could have thrown that rock—not to mention a lot of assholes who aren't teenagers," she said.

"I don't suppose you've been to our fine municipal swimming pool today have you, Mr. Moore?" Sheriff Lena asked.

"Nope, got my own pool," Duane said.

"It's drained for cleaning at the moment, which inspired a local grafitti artist to paint a sentiment on the bottom. Maybe you better go look."

Duane promptly did. The pool was nearly surrounded by wobbly old folks from the nearby nursing home. They were in bathrobes, mainly. A few had oxygen tanks.

All were looking at what was written on the bottom of the pool. What was written was:

RICH CUNT GO HOME!

One of the oxygen tankers, old man Jakes, who hadn't said a good word for anybody in several years, wobbled around the edge of the pool, in danger of falling in.

"It's what comes of educating the niggers," he said. "I said it long ago and I'll say it again."

"To my knowledge we have never educated a single Negro in this town, because there's none that live here," Duane said. "You don't know what you're talking about and you never have known. If you don't shut up I'll turn off your oxygen."

Old Mr. Jakes looked stunned.

"You shouldn't pick on Charlie, Duane, he's too old to know up from down," an old lady named Coolidge said.

"You're all old but it's no reason to lie," he said to the lady politely, "and I'm just a step or two behind you. It don't excuse prejudice."

Then he went to the hardware store, bought some paint remover and erased the graffiti from the bottom of the pool.

K.k. slater took the news matter-of-factly. She seemed neither happy to hear it, nor upset.

"The reason the very rich congregate in certain watering holes is because nobody really likes them except themselves, and sometimes not then. But the point of Aspen, Vail, Sun Valley, Long Island, West Palm, Malibu, Gstaad, the Hotel du Cap and so on is in those places the super-rich can congregate and not feel too exceptional. These places take in a lot of money by providing very rich people the illusion of normalcy.

"A few are normal and God are they boring," she went on.

"Maybe, but they probably don't throw rocks at people having dinner, or write nasty things in the bottom of swimming pools."

K.K. shrugged.

Dal was still not home, and it made Duane nervous. What if she just never came back? She may have liked working for Dickie but she could hardly have enjoyed Wichita Falls or Thalia. What if she stayed in Thailand?

Then one night when he was watching the Weather Channel he heard the back door open, and Dal walked in, carrying her small knapsack. When she saw him she gave him an affectionate hug and a kiss, smiling her sly, shy smile.

"You okay, Mr. Moore?"

"I was thinking we were on a first name basis," he mentioned.

"We are, but I've been away and I feel shy," Dal said. "Besides, I need to shower. Airplanes get filthier and filthier."

When she came out her hair was wet and she had wrapped a towel around her head. She made them tea.

"Have a good time?" he asked, as she handed him a spoon for his honey.

"Not very," Dal admitted. "My mother is going to die soon. Leaving her was hard. And my children don't know me very well, which is not right.

And a not very nice man in Bangkok offered me a job for much more money."

Duane had feared something like that might happen.

"I didn't take the job, but neither did I close the door. I told him I would have an answer for him in thirty days, and would have to give Dickie thirty days' notice if I should quit."

Duane felt the beginning of a great sadness but did not feel surprised. He had allowed himself to think of a life with Dal, while all the while knowing that it probably would not come to pass. He didn't have many years to offer her, and even if he was younger why would she want to live in such a miserable place?

Besides, it was merely normal that she would want to live closer to her family, and know her children better.

He said nothing but he felt Dal watching him.

"I think you are in love with me, Mr. Moore," she said. "Is that not true?"

"Yes, it's true," he said. "I am in love with you but I never much expected you'd want to spend your life in a place like this."

"You are right, I wouldn't," Dal said. "All the same you are a wonderful man and if I could live for the love of a man I would choose you."

"Thanks," Duane said.

"Do you know what Tuol Sleng is?" she asked.

Duane shook his head.

"It was a prison," she said. "A million Cambodians died there, or near there. My husband was tortured to death there. He was a teacher—only a teacher. In relation to Tuol Sleng I was one of the lucky ones. I was raped and tortured but not killed. One of the guards was my cousin. He helped me escape and I got to Thailand. My mother and two of my children made it, but not my sisters. They died, there in Tuol Sleng."

"A million people dying—it's hard to imagine," he said.

"I was sodomized with a hose, and worse things than that were done to me, Mr. Moore," Dal said, with a distant look in her eyes.

"Lenin or Stalin or somebody said that one death is a tragedy, a million deaths a statistic," she said shaking her head.

"I do not feel like a statistic," she said. "I felt like a woman who had been sent to hell. And I *was* sent to hell, along with my husband, two sisters and our children."

She was silent for a bit.

"And now I am bringing this hell to you, who love me and have been only kind to me. I will take the offer of the man in Bangkok but I wanted to tell you first. It is a lot of money but it is not for the money I am going, you know?"

Dal rubbed her eyes but did not cry.

"I need to be closer to my children, but that is not why I am going to take the offer, either."

"Why, then?" he asked. "Wanting to be closer to your family is only normal."

"But *I* am not normal, Duane," she said. "No one who went through Tuol Sleng is normal—though some pretend to be," she said.

"It is not my family I need to be closer to," she said. "I need to be closer to my ghosts, Mr. Moore. I hope you understand that."

45

"IT'S THE NATURE of the business, Daddy," Dickie said, a few days after Dal had left. "Anyone as good as Dal is going to get hired away."

"I know, I'm a grown man—I'll live."

"That's not a given," Dickie said.

"I guess I need to stop falling in love with these pretty analysts you bring in."

Dickie didn't answer—soon Duane left. The next day he got a letter from Dal, mailed from the Dallas–Fort Worth Airport. He opened it and propped it up against a teacup to read it.

> *Dear Duane—*
>
> *Do not shut out life because I am gone. It is odd that I should ever have been in Wichita Falls and Thalia but the good part of it was that we met. For reasons of my past I thought I must be formal with you—many Cambodians are formal. But my friendship with you will always be a solace—to me, and I hope to you.*
>
> *I hope you mend fences with your daughters—they are just confused, as is my own daughter, back home.*
>
> *To forgive is to survive. I know.*
>
> *Your friend always*
> *Dal*

Duane did not know who he needed to forgive, exactly—they had grown up as country girls and now were trying to be city girls—of course they made mistakes, but he did not feel that they were lost to him.

He was not even sure that Annie Cameron was lost to him, even if all that joined them was her anger. The fact that she was still angry troubled him, but it also meant that, in some measure, she was still there.

It was Dal, whom he loved most of all his women, who was not still there. Dal was gone forever—he felt it in his gut. He was a Texas working-man—it was odd indeed that computers and the effect they had on the oil business had brought women into his life that would never have been in his life even ten years ago. His wife Karla had her fatal car wreck just as the world changed. She had not been happy when Honor Carmichael came into his life and she would have been even more angry about the women who followed.

That night, for the first time that he could remember, Duane wondered how it would be just to go to sleep and not wake up. He did not want to do anything to effect his end, but if his eventual departure involved just going to sleep and quietly ceasing to live, that would, he thought, be ideal.

What had come as an idle thought became a frightening thought. He did not want to leave all his duties, all his friendships, in that way. He did not want to die at all—he would have to someday.

Of course he was sad that Dal was gone, but Willy wasn't gone, nor Dickie, nor his daughters, nor Honor, nor K.K., for that matter. Or Bobby Lee.

He still had people, he still had duties. Not going on would be a betrayal of all he believed.

Finally he went to sleep—and, when morning came, woke up.

I**N HIS SLEEP** Duane dreamed that he and Karla were working in the garden—it was a common dream with him, and, of course, annually they *had* worked in a garden, so the dream had an old basis.

When he woke the first thing he sensed was that someone was working in the garden—then he remembered that Stephanie, K.K.'s long-legged cook, had been invited to forage in the garden and take what she wanted. When he peeked out the window he saw that it was indeed Stephanie, wearing cutoffs, a Texas Rangers baseball cap and sandals. So far she had some turnips, some collard greens and several cucumbers in her basket.

Duane got into some clothes and wandered out.

"Hi, Mr. Moore, I'm out here pillaging," she said cheerfully. "I love turnips. Isn't it a fine day?"

It was a beautiful sunny day.

"What are you doing with yourself?" she asked.

"Working at being retired," he said. "It's kind of a full-time job."

"I'll never retire—people always need cooks," Stephanie said. "Of course I might change my mind if I met a real sexy guy. If that ever happens I plan to have a bunch of babies. I haven't attained orgasm yet but I'm still hopeful. The clitoris is supposed to have eight thousand nerve endings, but somehow the guys I date can never find very many of them."

When she bent to pick a cucumber he saw the valley between her young breasts, which were heavy, despite her slim build.

Stephanie, like Casey, was a heavy gum chewer—heavy enough that it made her breasts move a little. She looked at him, and picked up on where he was looking, but she didn't say anything for a while.

Duane remembered Dal's admonition—don't push life away. Here was life—young life.

"K.K.'s gone for the day, if that's what's stopping you," Stephanie said.

"I bet you'd like to see if you could find some of those nerve ends on my clitoris."

"Stephanie, I'm tempted, but I'm going to pass," he said.

"What?" she said, genuinely surprised. "You're going to pass up a free fuck with *me*?"

"Yes," Duane said.

"But why?"

"I don't know why," he admitted. "I honestly don't."

"Wow—I was lying about the orgasms," she said. "If that's what's worrying you, forget it. Given a reasonably hard dick I can come in about three minutes."

"Glad to hear it," Duane said, and turned toward the house.

"Hey, don't let it affect our friendship, Mr. Moore," Stephanie said.

"I won't."

"Come to dinner, we're having swordfish—K.K.'s bringing it from Dallas.

"Sounds good, I'll be there," Duane said.

STEPHANIE SLADE DID such a fine job of cooking for K.K. that soon invitations to dine at the penthouse were much coveted. Boyd Cotton came, on average, three times a week, and Duane had begun to eat there almost every night, usually with Bobby Lee in tow.

Boyd was contentedly running the nilgai operation now, while occasionally helping out with the Scottish cattle, which he still didn't really like.

K.K. had yet to deliver Hondo Honda's famous rifle to the Texas Ranger Hall of Fame—most nights she kept it on the counter in the penthouse.

"Would you shoot someone, K.K.?" Boyd asked one night.

"I'm probably capable of that," K.K. said. "It would depend on my mood. In truth there are not that many things I'm not capable of—though many of those things I'll never actually do.

"I come from an eye-for-an-eye part of the country," she reminded them.

K.K., annoyed by Bobby Lee at first, had finally taken to him. On nights when he had to stay on the guard tower she would have someone take one of Stephanie's meals out to him.

Bobby Lee's self-esteem, low for years, began to soar once K.K. began to pay him some attention.

"She's a real down-to-earth gal, once you get to know her," he claimed one day, a remark that caused both Boyd and Duane to snort.

"Bobby, she's a billionairess—how could she be down-to-earth?" Duane asked.

"And then there's her thoroughbreds," Boyd mentioned. "Nobody down-to-earth would risk their lives day after day riding crazy horses."

One day Duane discovered that Stephanie Slade, a city-bred girl, had never been to a rodeo. There was one in Olney that weekend and, on impulse, Duane agreed to take her.

Before the rodeo started the two of them were wandering around behind the chutes when they encountered a young cowboy Duane knew: Dwight Magee. Dwight was young, lean and good-looking, besides being probably the best calf roper in the area.

Duane spotted an oilman he wanted to gossip with a bit, so he left Stephanie with Dwight for a few minutes—when he came back and tried to find her he couldn't.

Calf roping was traditionally the second event, right after bareback riding. The event came and went, and Dwight Magee did not show up to rope his calf.

Stephanie Slade was never seen in that part of the country again.

"I could have told you she'd do that, if you'd asked me," K.K. said, later.

A year later Dwight Magee came limping back to the short grass country and quickly regained his high place in the local calf roping community.

Duane asked him once, casually, what had become of Stephanie Slade, only to have Dwight Magee walk away without answering.

NOT LONG AFTER Duane left Stephanie at the rodeo in Olney, he answered an ad in the Fort Worth paper and bought a cabin cruiser, which was duly delivered. It was in poor condition, but it floated.

"I guess that's about the last we'll see of you—us working people, that is," Bobby Lee said.

"No it isn't—I just want a boat I can sleep on," Duane said.

"What about that cabin you rebuilt for no good reason, at great expense?" Bobby asked.

"A cabin isn't a boat," Duane pointed out, patiently, he thought.

"If I feel like sitting on a hill I can stay in my new cabin," Duane said. "If I feel like being on the water, which I often do, I can sleep on my boat.

"It's even got two bunks—you could sleep over and we could lay a trot line," he added.

"I'm a little above trot line fishing," Bobby Lee said, remembering his record bass. But in a flash he changed his mind.

"Okay, sure," he said. "Next you'll have a yacht, I expect."

No yacht appeared, but the cabin cruiser eventually got repainted and repaired. While the work was being done Duane fulfilled a promise to his grandson and went to London.

Willy met him at Gatwick and took him into London on the Tube. The massiveness of the buildings in central London—Piccadilly, Westminster, the Strand, the various parks—all thrilled him. They rented a car, and Willy, by then unfazed by the fact that the English drove on the left, took him to Blenheim, Stonehenge, Chatsworth, Oxford, Cambridge and the Cotswolds. They visited several cathedrals.

Duane tried driving once but gave up at the first roundabout. They drove up to Edinburgh and then took a train back to London.

"What do you think, Grandpa?" Willy asked, once they were back in London.

"I think there was a lot of money here once," Duane said, indicating the buildings near the Victoria and Albert Museum, the only museum Willy insisted that they see.

"Yep, and some of it's still here," Willy said. "Though the aristocrats mostly don't have enough money to live in their own family houses."

"I'd like to see an aristocrat—maybe just once," Duane said.

"K.K.'s a kind of aristocrat," Willy told him. "She's probably as close as an American can get, except for one or two museum directors."

"I don't know K.K. well, but I don't think she's happy," Duane said.

"I've begun to think that maybe happiness is too much to ask," Willy said. "Though I've been pretty happy at Oxford."

"It's not too much to ask," Duane said. "It's just that it tends to be temporary. Your Granny and I were pretty happy for a good long time."

"But then you weren't," Willy said.

"Then we weren't," Duane agreed.

THE LONG FLIGHT home from Gatwick to Dallas interested Duane quite a lot. Willy had finished the first year of his Rhodes and was accompanying his grandfather back to Texas.

Near Greenland they looked down and saw icebergs. William spent most of his time writing and receiving e-mails. Crossing Canada took hours—Duane was quite surprised at how much Canada there turned out to be.

"I hope my mom doesn't rattle on about your Asian girlfriend," Willy said, with a sigh. He had not much wanted to leave England, even for the month he would be home.

"Your mother doesn't keep up very well. Dal was never my girlfriend and she left to take a job in Thailand a month ago. I miss her but her family's in Thailand and it's probably for the best."

"You can't really know, though," Willy said. "Only time can determine what's really for the best."

"See, you've become a philosopher, like you planned to," Duane said.

"I became a philosopher at about three, when I started trying to figure out why there was so much tension in our house—and it got worse when you started your walking."

"Did you ever figure it out—the reason for the tension?"

"Sure, it was a house full of lunatics," Willy said. "Even Granny seemed crazy a lot of the time.

"We're a family of hedonists," he added.

"Tell me again what a hedonist is?" Duane asked.

"People who spend their lives doing exactly what they want to do, regardless of the feelings and needs of others.

"I don't really include Granny in that," Willy said. "Sometimes Granny was totally responsible."

"I'm glad you're going back to England for your second year. I think England suits you."

"In some ways it's a broken culture, but it's a great culture."

Watching Illinois pass beneath him Duane began to think about his boat.

50

WHEN DUANE GOT home everybody asked him if he had snapshots of himself and Willy in all the new places he had been. They wanted, for some reason, to see him in a tourist-like context. They assumed he would come home with lots of souvenirs, but in fact he had neither snapshots nor souvenirs. Karla had always taken hundreds of pictures of everywhere they went—but Duane was not Karla.

"You didn't even take a camera?" K.K. said. "That's almost immoral. What is wrong with you?"

"Probably a lot," Duane said—"So much that I don't think I'd want a picture of it."

Indeed, it had never occurred to him to take a camera.

51

DUANE AND BOBBY LEE began to spend a lot of their spare time on Duane's newly painted and restored cabin cruiser.

"A boat needs a name," Bobby observed.

"Okay, let's call it the *Bobby Lee*," Duane said. "I've left it to you in my will anyway."

They were way out in the middle of Lake Kickapoo, hoping to avoid the swarms of mosquitoes that overhung the shores.

"Really?" Bobby Lee asked, stunned.

He grew misty-eyed at the thought that Duane was willing him the boat.

A fish jumped out of the water, arched and plopped back in.

"That was a three-pounder," Duane observed.

"Well, we didn't catch it, so who cares?"

He seemed nervous for some reason.

"What's wrong with you?" Duane asked. With Bobby, or with most people, it seemed better just to ask.

"Nothing," Bobby said. "I been dating Lena Loftis. We're thinking of tying the knot."

"Oh, you're just trying to round up a best man then," Duane said. "Sounds like a fine match to me. I'll be glad to be your best man."

"The truth of the matter is a little awkward," Bobby Lee said.

"How so?"

"We couldn't wait. We dug up a J.P. and got it done."

"Does the town know?"

"They will tomorrow, when the list of marriages comes out in the paper."

"You're a thrill a minute, Bobby," Duane said.

Then he got back to serious fishing.

"**I** WAS UP IN British Columbia once, fishing, and a guide told me that a grizzly bear could hide so well that you could be within three feet of him and not know it," Bobby Lee said.

"Three feet!" he insisted.

"That's the kind of information that would deter me from chasing off to British Columbia, fishing or no fishing," Duane said.

They were walking away from Boyd Cotton's funeral, a small funeral, attended by maybe twenty people. It was small because most of the cowboys and cattlemen Boyd had worked with were long dead themselves.

Boyd had been in the big rhino pasture, looking for two nilgai that had somehow slipped into it, when a large rhino burst out of a small mesquite thicket and tossed Boyd's quarter horse, with Boyd on it, several feet in the air. The horse turned in falling and landed on Boyd, killing him instantly.

The thicket was only an acre or two, but it was dense. Boyd took the rhino danger serious, and was watchful when he was in the big pasture. And yet neither Boyd nor his number-one quarter horse had sensed that nearly two tons of rhino was just a few yards away.

"Animals can do things we don't understand, like those bears in British Columbia," Duane reminded him.

K.K. Slater was in Mongolia when the death occurred. The quarter horse had to be put down too.

K.K. was trying to save a rare antelope, and also the wild horses of the Gobi.

She could not make it back for the funeral but the first thing she did, on her return, was visit Boyd's grave, which was on a rise near his little house. His father, mother and sister were also buried there. At his funeral they had hung his spurs over a little cross, but the spurs were stolen within a week.

"I hope an admirer took them, at least," K.K. said.

"Probably just a thief," Duane said.

DUANE BEGAN TO notice a tone in Honor Carmichael's voice that hadn't been there before. She sounded weaker, for some reason. Not much weaker, but certainly not as strong as she had seemed on her visit to Thalia. Honor had always had a robust voice, calm and rich. In his days as her patient he had come to like her voice before he really liked her.

Now, something was off. He felt a nagging worry.

"Are you okay?" he asked one day, gathering his nerve.

There was a silence on the line.

"I was hoping you wouldn't ask that," she said.

"Well, are you?" he repeated.

"If you must know I'm dying," Honor said. "Pancreatic cancer—a bad one."

"Uh-oh," Duane said.

His instinct had been right, although he hadn't expected Honor to have something fatal.

"Ever notice how when your friends start dying there's a kind of stampede for the door?" Honor said. "Pretty soon half your acquaintance is gone."

"What are you going to do about it?" he asked.

"Not too much—drink a lot and take drugs," she said. "I have a very compliant, nonpuritanical doctor. He's given me what will ease me."

"I might go to Paris, but probably not," she went on. "I've seen a lot of Paris."

"I guess that means you won't be coming here," he said.

"I won't, honey—no," she said. "Long Island's not a bad place to die—and I have good friends here, and there's the sea. Nothing more soothing than old Mother Sea."

She sighed. "Right now I'm tired, though—I'll talk to you in a while."

Duane hung up. He waited two weeks and called again, only to be told that Honor was in a coma.

Two days later she died.

There was a small service in Vernon, Honor's birthplace, that Duane went to. The only survivor was an old deaf aunt who could not be made to realize who Duane was or why he was there. The crowd was an oil patch crowd, not a ranching crowd. Rain began to splatter the mourners as they hurried to their cars and pickups, and a ferocious hailstorm caught Duane as he was driving back to Thalia. He finally stopped under an overpass, to let it hail itself out. Before it ended the whole highway might have been covered with snow.

"Bad news for the wheat farmers," Duane said as he drove home.

"So now you've lost your sounding board," K.K. said, when she was back from Mongolia, where she had gone three times. She was feeding him supper at her penthouse.

"It's a wonder I ever went to her in the first place," Duane said. "Back then it was a big deal for a man to go to a shrink. My wife hated it like crazy, and the home folks could talk of nothing else. Successful oilmen weren't supposed to get disturbed.

"Honor helped me a lot," he added.

"She must have been nice, but the two women she lived with weren't one bit nice," K.K. said. "They were cunts, both of them. One had talent and one didn't, but they were both cunts."

"Honor did her best to polish me," Duane said.

"She made you less provincial," K.K. said. "She saw a rough diamond and rubbed it a little."

Just then a single car light came along the road from the east.

"It's nice to be in a place where there's only one car on the road at night," K.K. said.

Somewhat to their surprise the one car light belonged to Willy Moore's modest Honda. Willy was driving and he had brought a passenger.

"Hi, ma'am," Willy said, when he and his friend reached the penthouse. "I hear you need a sculptor and I've brought you one. Lucas Hawkins."

Lucas was skinnier than Willy, and had a quiet smile. They both shook K.K.'s hand.

"Lucas Hawkins? *The* Lucas Hawkins . . . the toast of New York?"

"Oh, not hardly," Lucas said.

"He means not yet," Willy said.

In the sorrow over Boyd Cotton's passing they had paid only a little attention to the fact that Colby Jordan, the famous sculptor K.K. had wanted to do the statue of Hondo, had been killed in a car wreck near Cyril, Oklahoma.

Now here was a possible replacement, at least in Willy Moore's opinion.

"Such a small world—how did you two meet?" K.K. asked.

"Same prep school," Willy said. "I think our parents wanted to get rid of us at the same time, for the same reasons."

"They shipped us off," Lucas agreed.

"Lucas is already famous, and I'm not," Willy said.

"Hey, you're a Rhodes Scholar," Lucas reminded him.

K.K. was watching the two young men with a smile. She liked them and soon dished them up some linguine with scallops.

"Don't you love the *jeunesse dorée*? she asked Duane.

"I might if I knew what it meant," Duane said.

"Golden youth, Grandpa," Willy said. "Just another way of saying overprivileged kids. But Lucas really is a good sculptor—he's even shown in Venice.

"Can Lucas stay with us at your house, while he sees if he can get this job?" Willy asked.

"If not there's plenty of room here," K.K. said. "I'll do just about anything for the *jeunesse dorée*."

K.K., Lucas and Willy proceeded to talk up a storn. Most of the talk was over Duane's head.

Duane got sleepy and went home.

Far into the night, he heard the boys come in.

55

L UCAS HAWKINS SPENT the whole of the next day looking at his poten-
tial site. He walked around and around the courthouse and even got
permission to go up under the roof. After that he sat on the south side of
K.K.'s penthouse and looked some more.

Willy, meanwhile, was at Duane's house, reading Descartes.

K.K., who, for the moment, was her own cook, gave them a cold pasta
lunch. While they were eating, Sheriff Lena Loftis showed up —she had
kept her own name when she married Bobby Lee. Since there was lots of
pasta, she had a plate.

Lena Loftis kept looking at Lucas Hawkins, and he looked back just as
hard.

"I know you from somewhere," she said, finally.

"You look familiar too—where'd you grow up?" he asked.

"Crowell," she said.

"I'm from Floydada," Lucas said.

"You guys used to beat us in football every year— you were the field
goal kicker, weren't you?"

"By golly, I was," Lucas said.

"You kicked the field goal that beat us the one year we thought we'd go
to state," she said. "The whole town was depressed for two weeks."

"I kicked that field goal and then I got shipped off to prep school and
never kicked again," Lucas said.

"Of course there's a lot to be depressed about in Crowell," Lena said.
"You make those skinny scuptures, don't you? I saw something about you
in *Texas Monthly*."

"That's me—the American Giacometti, they called me. Embarrassing.

"But I'd love to put a statue or two on that courthouse lawn," Lucas
said.

Lena made a face and shook her head.

"Nope—the town has mobilized against you. No statues permitted, K.K.'s money will be refunded. It don't help that Crowell's beat us at football ten years running now."

"Wait a minute," K.K. said. "Lucas is an internationally recognized sculptor. Why are they mobilizing against him?"

Lena sighed.

"It's really you they're mobilizing against," Duane said. "It's been coming and now it's here."

"The courthouse is public property," Lena said. "I think they might have accepted a John Wayne–like sculture of Hondo, but a skinny statue by Floydada's most deadly placekicker is not going to fly.

"The fact is Hondo Honda was not that well liked, either," Lena added.

"And didn't care," Duane said.

"No—but where Lucas is concerned I think you ought to remember that this is the land of metal art. Calves, longhorns, cutting horses. That kind of thing. Thanks for the pasta, K.K."

Lucas didn't seem surprised or particularly nonplussed.

"There went my loft in Brooklyn," he said.

"Maybe not," Duane said. "I know of a fine place you could put your sculptures. And Moore Drilling owns it. It's a section with a nice little bluff across the road from the Rhino Ranch. You could have statues on one side of the road and rhinos on the other."

Willy slouched in about that time, with his paperback Descartes in one hand.

"Do you mean it?" Lucas asked.

"Grandpa always means it," Willy said.

K.K. Slater did not say a word. After a few more minutes she got up and left the table.

"Cogito ergo pissed," Willy said.

56

THE NEXT MORNING both boys slept till noon. Duane, long accustomed to the nocturnal habits of the young, just let them sleep.

He called K.K. several times during the morning but only got her machine. No doubt she was angry about the town's decision not to permit the statue. So was he—but there might be ways to fight the decision if she wanted to.

When the *jeunesse dorée* finally got up they ate a lunch consisting mostly of French toast. When they were finished he drove them to the site he had in mind, the little section with the nice bluff that K.K.'s men had tried to buy back when things began to get a little topsy-turvy in Thalia.

They parked and walked around the little piece of bottom land before climbing the bluff. In the distance, across the road, they could see three rhinos grazing.

Lucas Hawkins had been very polite but reserved, until he saw the rhinos. Then his face lit up.

"Oh wow!" he said. "Somehow the notion that there were really rhinos in my part of the country didn't seem quite real, until now."

Lucas walked off and stood by himself at the edge of the little bluff, looking at the rhinos in the distance. Then he sat down and just looked, and looked some more.

"Don't be impatient with him, Grandpa," Willy said. "He has to look and look before he knows what he might want to build. He may sit and look at those rhinos for two hours."

"So what do we do?"

"Just leave him—he can walk to town if he wants to. I thought we might go to Mike and Tommy's."

Before they left Lucas came back to the pickup.

"Can I get closer to the rhinos?" he asked.

"Probably," Duane said. "But I'm not sure. Since Bobby Lee quit his job with Rhino Enterprises I'm not that clear what the rules are."

All Duane knew for sure is that the sturdy pipe fences had been put up, after which no rhinos were spotted near Amarillo, or anywhere else except Thalia.

The only person he knew who might know what the rules were—other than the present team, again Australian—was K.K. This time when he called she answered.

"The young sculptor is interested in the rhinos," he told her. "Can you make a call and get us on the preserve?"

"Better yet, I'll come take you on," she said.

"Might just be Lucas—Willy and I might go to Mike and Tommy's."

"Fine, I was going to try and lose you two anyway—or at least lose you," she said. "Then I'd have the little darlings all to myself."

"And if I can have young Lucas to myself for an hour, so much the better."

"You sound like you're going to eat him."

"I might," K.K. said.

57

"**L**UCAS IS REALLY at ease with rich women," Willy pointed out. They were returning from a good light meal at Mike and Tommy's.

"I suppose it's a handy trait," Duane said.

"Sure is—who do you think buys the work of young artists? Mainly rich women."

"How'd you get to be so self-possessed?" Duane asked, changing the subject.

"It could be that you just see me in my self-possessed moments," Willy said. "Or maybe being with you makes me seem more self-possessed than I really am."

"I don't know if that's true," Duane said.

"I'm trying to be a philosopher, remember?" Willy said. "Trying to figure out what—if anything—is true is what I do."

"Would you admit that you're more poised than most people your age?"

"Oh sure, but that's because I grew up in a family of nut cases," Willy said. "I decided to be the sane, calm one, and I decided that on the day you stopped your pickup and began your walks—I think you were really just walking away from everybody and I didn't know that you'd be back."

"It seemed like the most reasonable thing I could do at the time," Duane told him. "And besides that, I was tired of being in pickups.

"I saw it as a revolt against the pickup," he added. "In the short term I won but in the long term I lost."

"Which is proven by the fact that it's a pickup we're riding in," Willy said.

LUCAS HAWKINS AND K.K. Slater spent the afternoon and all the next day looking at rhinos.

In the afternoon Willy became bored with Thalia and drove back to Dallas. Soon he would be flying back to England.

"Is Lucas a good hitchhiker?" Duane asked.

"No but he's resourceful," Willy said. "I'm his friend, not his keeper. K.K. likes him and she can just summon a car or a plane to take him wherever he needs to go."

As usual, Duane felt a little droop in spirit when Willy left. He was also a little disappointed that Lucas seemed more interested in rhinos than he was in scattering sculptures on Moore Drilling's property, though he hadn't formally ruled it out.

Lucas made it clear that he was nothing if not independent. He liked K.K., but did not solicit her opinion, or Duane's.

"He can be haughty, Lucas," Willy had said, and he was right. Lucas *was* haughty and yet he was friendly as well.

"It's just that *I* have to find the spot and decide what I think should go on it," he explained to Duane.

"I like that bluff, though," he added. "If you'll give me a year to think about it I bet I can do something."

"The bluff has got a year," Duane said.

"I'll be back from time to time—next time I'll bring a camera," Lucas promised.

Then he called himself a car from Wichita Falls and was quietly driven away.

59

I N THE ABSENCE of any pressing duties—Duane would not see that he would ever have pressing duties again—he began to spend more and more time on his boat, now officially named the *Bobby Lee*, mostly just drifting around the muddy waters of Lake Kickapoo. On the weekends Bobby Lee often joined him, but during the week his wife, Sheriff Lena Loftis, often drafted him as an unofficial deputy. If there was a car wreck on one of the county highways—and few days passed without at least one car wreck—Bobby Lee was forced to put on an orange vest and get out cones, and direct traffic around the crash scene. He didn't like these duties and was often testy with any driver who did not immediately obey his instructions.

Once and once only K.K. Slater came on the boat with Duane. She brought some brandy and drank it as they drifted here and there.

"I guess it's time to face the fact that things didn't really work out for me here," she said. "You're about the only local who likes me and sometimes I'm not so sure about you."

"I like you fine," Duane said. "But you aren't really going to stay here, are you?"

"No, but I thought I would, at first," she told him. "I do like the rhinos and I do think it's a valuable program. But when you start something like this, and invest your time and energy in it, pretty soon you discover that you're just a bureaucrat, running a bureaucracy, directing people who come to know more about the project than you do. I'm not like Miriam Rothschild, who really is a world-renowned expert on the flea."

She sighed.

"I'm finally just a rich dilettante," she said, draining her brandy.

"Well," Duane said, but went no farther. K.K. was right about herself and he couldn't think of a thing to say that might cheer her up.

"After all I did actually *marry* Hondo. What does that say about me?"

She drained her brandy.

"Sometimes I wish you'd shown some interest, Duane," she said.

"We're on my fishing boat, about to watch a beautiful sunset," he said. "I know it's just scenery, but scenery's mostly what I have to offer, these days."

"I suspect you're too modest," K.K. said.

60

"**I** NEED YOU, DUANE! I need you bad," Annie said—it was late at night. Duane was on his boat. He had invited Bobby Lee, but Bobby was, as he put it, on a short leash; his wife the sheriff had caught him watching porn on her computer.

"Seems like this issue has come up before in your life," Duane recalled.

"Yeah, but then my wife was *doing* the porn," Bobby Lee said. "I blame all this on my penile implant."

So Duane was alone on his boat when Annie called.

"Where are you and what's wrong?" he asked.

"I'm in Wickenburg, Arizona, in rehab for meth addiction, and I don't think I can stand it," Annie said. "I was addicted before I even married you—though I shook it off for a while. In Arizona I got it from that carpenter we had. You didn't even notice when I was high."

Actually Duane had noticed a few times, but he had failed to peg her highs to meth. He had blamed it on pot, or maybe cocaine, even her angers and fits, which were frequent.

"How long have you been in?"

"Three days, don't ask questions, just come and get me."

Duane knew a good bit about rehab, since all his children and some of his grandchildren had been in at least once—not to mention maybe a score of his employees. He knew for sure that a person in rehab for meth needed to stay longer than three days.

"Annie, if it's meth, three days is not much of a try," he said.

"I don't give a fuck—come and get me out."

"Did you commit yourself, or did someone commit you?"

"Why is that any of your business?" Annie asked. "You're the only one who ever really loved me—why do you have to ask questions when I'm desperate! This is me, Duane, your sweetie—just come get me out.

"Don't sit there in that rat hole and think about stuff—just come!"

He remembered that Honor Carmichael had mentioned that she thought Annie had remarried.

"Did your husband commit you?" he asked, finally.

"Go to hell, you fucking prick!" Annie said, and hung up.

SOON ENOUGH, DUANE'S conscience began to bother him. He had loved Annie deeply once—perhaps at some level he still did love her. She had her failings but also her virtues. She had been very sweet to him, many times. Perhaps he should go to Wickenburg. He had no intention of helping her escape or anything, but perhaps he should go see her.

K.K. was still in town. A very cute baby rhino had been born a few days earlier—the little rhino was female, and the staff wanted to name her K.K., so K.K. stayed for the christening and good photo ops were had by all.

There was a large crowd in the little grandstand that had been built as a viewing station. Many in the crowd came to see the baby but a solid group of tourists came in the belief that Double Aught was still alive and would come trotting back someday.

So high was Double Aught's popularity among those who had mainly never seen him that another movie was planned, also to be called *The Legend of Double Aught*—but the production kept being postponed.

It was evening before he got a moment with K.K.—she had brought in some Kobe beef and cooked it herself. It was over dinner that he told her about Annie.

"I think I see your pattern, Duane," K.K. said. "Honor Carmichael is dead, so you're asking me what you would have asked her, which is basically whether to go to Wickenburg or not to go.

"You know what happens to meth addicts—just look down the street. Whoever threw that rock at us was probably doing meth."

Duane looked and saw several teenagers sitting on the courthouse lawn, smoking. One, now jobless, had been a fine high school quarterback. Now, like most of his companions, he was a meth head.

"I guess I better go," Duane said. "I know I probably can't help her, but I might always regret it if I don't try."

"That's right," K.K. said. "That's exactly right."

"I WAS AT A rodeo once, in Wickenburg," Bobby Lee said. "That event occurred many years ago."

Bobby Lee had invited himself on the long car trip to Arizona. Lena had agreed to this plan, the emotional temperature being still rather high at their house.

"There's some pretty fair scenery in New Mexico and Arizona," Lena said, when she handed Bobby over. "It might take my husband's mind off his penile implant for a while."

Starting from Thalia, it took them a full day to hit the good scenery. Duane had always wanted to cross the Rockies, so they went to Denver and crossed on I-70, which took them so high that Bobby Lee's ears popped. Then they coasted down toward southwestern Colorado and stayed north of Phoenix and on to Wickenburg.

"How'd you do in the rodeo here?" Duane asked.

"Oh, I just rode in the Grand Entry," Bobby said. "Other than that, I don't rodeo."

Duane left Bobby Lee in the motel room when he went out to the famous rehab facility, where many movie stars had been treated for a variety of addictions.

When he told the recepionist that he had once been Annie Cameron's husband, and wanted to visit if possible, the woman behind the reception desk looked stricken.

"I'm sorry to be the one to have to tell you this," she said, "but Annie Cameron is dead. It was in the local paper yesterday."

Duane felt a droop or a catch in his breastbone, but he did not really feel surprised—not really.

"I guess you had a long drive for nothing," the receptionist said.

"Not for nothing—but could you tell me what happened?"

"It was kinda like *Thelma and Louise*," the receptionist said. "Miss

Cameron got out somehow and stole a car. She got somewhere up on the Hopi Reservation and, I guess, picked up a hitchhiker. I guess they went north until they were pretty high up and then ran off one of the mesas—I think it was Second Mesa."

"Neither of them lived?"

"Neither of them lived—I guess her family came and got her. The funeral was yesterday, in California."

Later Duane checked his messages to see if anyone in the family had called him.

No one had.

"THAT'S TWO WOMEN you've lost to car wrecks—why are we going this way?" Bobby Lee asked. They were going north, on a very lonely road, toward the great mesas of Hopi.

"I'd like to see where she died—I'll put up a cross."

They were in a part of the West where death on the highway was so common that they even sold roadside crosses at the convenience stores. There was quite a variety.

They did find the place where Annie and her hitchhiker friend went off the road—it was near a Hopi village. They had not sailed off the mesa the way Thelma and Louise sailed into the Grand Canyon—but they had driven, apparently at high speed, into a narrow arroyo near the cliff's edge. Duane put up two crosses, one for Annie and one for her passenger. The paper said the passenger was an Inuit, a tribe from the Arctic. What he was doing on the lonely road south of Hopi nobody knew, though it was learned that he had been released from the Gallup jail only a few days before his fatal meeting with Annie.

Duane had kept a tiny picture of Annie in his wallet for many years— he took it out and pinned it to the cross with a cactus needle.

"This is about the saddest place I've ever been," Bobby Lee said. "There's nothing but a big empty here. Would there be any town I could fly home from? I sure miss my Lena."

Duane saw that Bobby Lee was genuinely distressed—he was trembling, in fact. Duane drove straight to Flagstaff and flew Bobby home.

"Ain't you coming?" Bobby asked.

"Not today," Duane said. "I feel like wandering a bit."

64

W HEN DUANE LEFT the Flagstaff airport he had no firm idea about what he was going to do. He was in his pickup—it was not a rental car he could just turn in. He could easily have found a driveaway company in Phoenix and turned it over to them, but he and Annie had once gone to Phoenix for a wedding and Duane hated the place so that he never wanted to go back.

What he did know was that he didn't want to be in Thalia for a while. He had his fishing equipment with him, but had not fished; he had always meant to learn fly-fishing someday and had an expensive rod and some lures—but he did not feel like learning fly-fishing just then.

He couldn't get Annie's pointless death off his mind. For some reason he felt like staying close to where she met her end. Why this was he didn't know, but it was the one clear feeling he had. For three nights he stayed in a motel in Tuba City, driving back to the death site every day.

He had never seen Monument Valley, except in movies of course, so he drove to it and idled around the great buttes for a day. There he picked up an old white-bearded hitcher who called himself Desert Johnny, who said he needed to get to Moab as soon as possible. Having nothing else to do, Duane took him, listening without comment to Desert Johnny's endless tales of his life as a traditional hobo.

Duane was just as glad when they got to Moab and he could let the old man out. A little later that day he learned from a woman at a gas station that Desert Johnny was actually quite well off.

"It's more like he just don't fit with the modern age," the woman said.

Duane wondered if *he* fit with the modern age—or any age.

From Moab, Duane made his way to the Canyon de Chelly, which turned out to be one of the most beautiful places he had ever seen. It was near a town called Chinle—the woman who checked him into the motel was Navaho and seemed more hostile than not. Later, when he talked to

K.K. about the Canyon de Chelly she told him about the sad history of the place—what struck him as saddest was Kit Carson, on orders from higher up, cutting down the Navahos' two thousand peach trees, reason enough, more than a hundred and fifty years later, to explain hostility on the part of the Navaho clerk.

The next day he took the Park Service tour of the canyon from the bottom—he felt he had never spent a more interesting day. When he got home he meant to read about several of the places he had seen, but particularly the Canyon de Chelly.

Later he remembered that Annie Cameron's mother had particularly urged him to see the Canyon de Chelly. It was the nicest thing any member of Annie's family had ever done for him.

DUANE DRIFTED AROUND eastern Arizona, northern New Mexico and western Colorado for several days. He admired the great bulk of Shiprock, before drifting south to the I-40, where he toured Acoma, the Sky City. The old women of Acoma sold beautiful pots but did not seem too friendly, either.

After much consideration, Duane bought two small pots, one for K.K. and the other for Lena Loftis.

Then he went home. He had several nice pictures of Annie—he had the best one framed and put it on his mantelpiece at the big house. Another, just as appealing, he put on his boat.

Bobby Lee was the first to notice this flowering of photographs of Annie Cameron.

"You didn't get along with her for shit when she was alive," he said. "Why all the pictures now?"

"Why not?" Duane asked.

Bobby was silent.

"I still hope to learn to mind my own business someday," he said.

"I don't mind your asking," Duane said. "Small-town people almost never mind their own business. Gossip is one of the things that keeps them alive, I guess."

"I guess you really miss Annie—it probably wasn't all bad," Bobby said. "Eve ate that apple and fucked us all, though."

"I don't lay Annie's death on Eve," Duane said. "I should have got there quicker."

After that conversation Duane bought a good many staples, including some whiskey, and for a time retired to his boat, the *Bobby Lee*. Usually he breakfasted at Mike and Tommy's; for reading material he made do with the fishing magazines he could buy at the bait shop.

His main visitor, Bobby Lee, despite being at the moment unemployed, had acquired a BlackBerry and consulted it frequently.

"This thing can help you keep right up with the sports news, or the oil news, either."

"You might have noticed that I retired," Duane pointed out. "I did it mainly to get away from news."

"It takes all kinds, I guess."

"I would dispute that," Duane said. "I think there are a few kinds we could do without."

"You mean like Hondo, or who?"

"No, Hondo wasn't so bad. He wasn't rude. It's rude behavior I can't tolerate."

"Oh, you mean like people making jokes about my penile implant?"

"That's exactly what I mean," Duane said.

66

DUANE SOON GREW to like living on his boat. He considered buying a genuine houseboat and living on it, but soon rejected that notion. What he had was enough.

Little by little he ceased to mingle much with people in Thalia, though he did soon notice that most of the people he *did* mingle with were younger than himself—they were the sons and daughters of people he had lived his life with. His own contemporaries were mostly buried now in the grim little cemeteries northwest of town.

With the death of Jenny Marlow he lost his last real intimate in Thalia, other than Bobby Lee. And with the death of Honor Carmichael he had lost his last real intimate among the females of the world. At times K.K. Slater almost became an intimate, but then K.K. could drop the screen in an instant, fly away and not be seen for six months.

One day, to his surprise, Annie's sister Mary did call. Mary had always seemed a lot less walled off than the rest of the Camerons.

"We buried poor Annie in Tiburon," she told him. "We used to sort of own Marin County but now we don't. It has a nice cemetery— go visit Annie anytime you like."

Duane said he would do that—indeed, he meant to do that. But he never went, though he did look up Tiburon on the road atlas. He had heard that California traffic was bad. Having lost two wives to car wrecks he decided to avoid the risk of joining them just then.

The Rhino Ranch continued to make a good deal of news. The breeding program was working—six rhino calves had been born on the preserve so far.

Still, many of the reporters who came to the Rhino Ranch managed to track Duane to his boat and ask him about Double Aught.

All Duane could do was shrug. He had no more idea than anyone else where Double Aught was, or if he was alive.

There were millions of hunters in the West and Midwest, any one of whom might do like the first good old boys from Durango, Colorado, who had seen Double Aught and been unable to resist shooting him— just as the two Germans had shot the most famous elephant in Africa. It could have happened ten miles from Thalia, on some back road—and who would know? Duane himself had stopped believing that Double Aught was alive—but still, he wasn't sure.

But then one day a perky, cute young female reporter came confidently down to his boat, and introduced herself as Nattie Grimble. She had dark hair, cut short, and wore a polo shirt and cutoffs—it seemed to Duane that nearly all young and attractive women had adopted cutoffs as their daily garb. In his early days, he recalled, women's legs were usually white—nowadays they mainly seemed to be tanned, and nicely so.

Besides the good legs Nattie Grimble had a cute, turned-up nose, and lovely brown eyes. Duane liked her immediately and invited her and her tape recorder onto his boat.

"I'm from Abilene," she announced. "I bet you've been there."

"Everybody in the oil business has been there," he said.

"Don't worry, I know Abilene sucks, Mr. Moore," Nattie said. "I really just came out here to see if you'd get drunk with me."

She took a fifth of bourbon out of her bag and put it on the table by her tape recorder.

"I'm a little shocked," he admitted. "You don't really look like the drinking type."

"Oh, I'm not," she said. "But I'm looking for a story and I'm told you can hallucinate that famous old rhino when you're drunk."

"Nattie, he was a *real* rhino—I never had to hallucinate him, and I never did."

"Then a lot of people in Thalia have been telling me lies," she said. "Most of them say you can hallucinate that rhino when you're drunk."

"They don't know me real well," Duane told her.

"Shucks," Nattie said. "How often do you shave, Mr. Moore?"

"When I'm batching, not often," he admitted.

"I want to at least get a picture of you on your boat and you'd just look so much better if you shaved."

Amused, Duane obliged her. Very soon he was clean-shaven, and Nattie Grimble took about twenty pictures of him. Then she searched until she found two clean glasses and poured each of them a modest drink.

"I put ice in mine," Duane said. "Water it down a little."

He offered her ice but she declined.

"You could make ice from filthy water and die of *E. coli*," she informed him.

"Caution never hurts," Duane said.

"Oh, caution can hurt," Nattie said. "Look at me. I'm so afraid I'll have sex with the wrong guy that I end up never having sex at all.

"My friends say I'm the last virgin," she added.

When she said it in her brash little voice Duane was flooded with déjà vu—Annie Cameron had said almost exactly the same thing to him once.

"Oh, I doubt you're quite the last," he told her— and then despite himself his eyes spilled over and tears washed his cheeks.

"Oh my God, I didn't mean to make you cry, Mr. Moore," Nattie said. "After all, my virginity is not your problem, it's mine, or maybe my boyfriend's."

"It's just the timing," he said. "A young woman I was once married to was killed in a car wreck. What you said reminded me of her."

"Oh gosh, here's some Kleenex," Nattie said, handing him some.

Duane could not remember when he had seen such an appealing girl.

"I'm just going to gulp down this whiskey and hike it on out of here."

"Please don't," Duane said.

"Just don't," he added.

"But why not? I spoiled your morning, didn't I?"

"No, you made my morning," Duane insisted.

He stopped crying and wiped his eyes again with the tissues.

"Okey-doke then, I'll stay—you might hallucinate that rhino once you're a little drunk. It might just happen in spite of yourself."

They dipped glasses and touched glasses and drank.

"We each made a new friend," Nattie said.

"Just in time too," Duane said.

Nattie didn't quite know what he meant, but she drank with him anyway.

67

AFTER THEY FINISHED the fifth of Jack Daniel's, Duane, who was not drunk at all, watched Nattie indulge in her passion for cleaning. In this case what she cleaned was the *Bobby Lee*. He had always liked bold women and Nattie Grimble was nothing if not bold.

"Mr. Moore, your sheets are rancid," she informed him. "Is there a laundrymat anywhere near? I'll worry myself sick over you if I have to think of you sleeping on those rancid sheets."

"I've got a good washing machine at my home in town," he said. "We can take 'em in and you can wash them there, if you really mean to go to that trouble."

"I do mean to—this whole boat is filthy," she told him. "Once we do the sheets I'm going to come back and do the rest of the boat, if you'll let me."

On the way to town they stopped at the Asia Wonder Deli, an establishment of which, at first, Nattie Grimble was deeply skeptical.

"Why would it be here?" she wondered. "We don't even have good Asian food in Abilene."

"It's here because this is where Mike and Tommy wanted to put it," he told her.

"Is it clean?" Nattie asked. "This is real difficult country for a person who likes to be clean.

"Besides, most people who run delis don't have much knowledge of hygiene."

But Mike and Tommy did not let Duane down. They laid out their best, spotlessly, and Nattie Grimble ate a huge amount. Tommy saw to it that she had fresh chopsticks for every course.

"Shoot, they don't even do that in San Francisco," Nattie said. "I'm going to tell the *Texas Monthly* food guy about you two. He used to be my boyfriend.

"Oh, Benny," Mike said. "He come often. He gave us four stars."

"Some of the people who write for the *Monthly* don't love Texas that much," she said.

"But you do?" Duane asked.

"You bet I do," Nattie said. "Where else could I meet a man who can hallucinate a rhino but sleeps on rancid sheets?" she asked. "I've dealt with the sheets—boy were they rancid," Nattie said.

"Thanks," Duane said.

68

NATTIE WENT BACK and gathered up everything that could be washed off the *Bobby Lee*, and followed Duane into town.

One look at his washer and dryer and the rancid factor reared its head again.

"Gosh, Mr. Moore, these machines are so old they ought to be in a museum—they're kind of too funky to use," Nattie insisted.

Then Nattie made a rapid tour of the house and came back with a huge mass of towels which she insisted were also in the rancid category.

They heard a car drive up and Willy Moore walked in. His hair was longish, but very clean, as were his jeans and T-shirt.

Willy looked at Nattie and Nattie looked at Willy and, as time was to prove, something clicked. As soon as Nattie stuffed the towels into the questionable washing machine she and Willy began to talk about their favorite bands.

"Want some wine, Nattie?—I brought some chianti," Willy asked.

Nattie immediately accepted some wine.

Duane, who had been vaguely wondering whether Nattie might have romantic designs on him, immediately stopped wondering. Willy and Nattie couldn't take their eyes off each other, and, for the next fifty years, rarely did. They fought fiercely but cleanly as they went through life.

While they were debating the merits of various bands, none of whom Duane had ever heard of, he slipped out and began to weed his garden—or, as he liked to think of it, *their* garden, for he still considered that Karla Laverne Moore was his helpmate in anything involving gardening.

Except for a few lingering blister bugs on the tomatoes, the garden was in pretty good shape. He leaned on his hoe and looked into the distance, toward the Rhino Ranch—he looked a long time, but no Double Aught was there.

Willy wrote a book on Wittgenstein and Husserl that made him instantly famous in philosophical circles; he became a Harvard fellow, taught at several great universities and, always musical, in his middle years began to compose—fugues and requiems, mostly. Nattie got a degree in sports journalism from Boston College and was soon broadcasting women's basketball, softball, track and whatever else turned up; their children grew up in locker rooms and broadcast studios, where they came to know many famous athletes and other celebrities.

They came to Thalia frequently—the sight of them made Duane deeply proud.

Nearly ten years after Willy and Nattie met and hit it off, Duane Moore quietly keeled over dead while laying a trot line. A fisherman found him within the hour.

At the modest funeral—most people living in Thalia scarcely knew Duane Moore—he was just an old man they might see at the post office— Bobby Lee Baxter, his sparse hair then white, sobbed like a baby.

"I never meant to outlive that man," he said to Willy. "What will I do now?"

"Keep on keeping on," Willy advised.

K.K. Slater came to the funeral. She was warm to Willy's family, and also to Bobby Lee.

Then she was driven back to the North Gate and got into her brand-new Cessna.

Watched by three rhinos and several assistants, K.K. got in her new plane, rose, circled toward Thalia and, as she circled over the graveyard, dipped her wing.

As far as anyone knew, she was never in Thalia again.